The Wasties

The Wasties

FREDERICK REUSS

Pantheon Books, New York

All rights reserved under International and Pan-American
Copyright Conventions. Published in the United States by
Pantheon Books, a division of Random House, Inc., New
York, and simultaneously in Canada by Random House of
Canada Limited, Toronto.

Pantheon Books and colophon are registered trademarks of
Random House, Inc.

Library of Congress Cataloging-in-Publication Data

Reuss, Frederick, 1960–
The wasties / Frederick Reuss.
p.   cm.
ISBN 0-375-42071-1
1. English teachers—Fiction. 2. Mute persons—Fiction.
3. Childishness—Fiction. I. Title.

PS3568.E7818 W37 2002
813'.54—dc21   2001055450

www.pantheonbooks.com

Book design by Virginia Tan

Printed in the United States of America

First Edition

2 4 6 8 9 7 5 3 1

In memory of my father

The Wasties

I have the wasties.

The wasties is what I call it. There are probably about four thousand different names for it but I don't like to pronounce most of them, much less try to understand what they really mean. The wasties is a disease of the soul and you don't have to have a theistic bone in your body to get it. There are those pedantic types who say it's not a disease, it's a "condition." For God's sake! Why bother making such distinctions? When you've got the wasties everything is perfect and nothing matters, sort of like Buddhism—except for those with the wasties there aren't any doctrinal outs. I call the wasties a disease of the soul because it envelops the whole being of a person and is imposed from within. There's nothing you can do about it. A condition is something imposed on you from without, something you can point to—like capitalism. But I have a disease of the soul. I call it the wasties. You can't see it. All you can do is feel the effects.

Lots of people have the wasties. The doctors say it's serious. All you can say to such people—well, there's not much you can say to such people. They've been too thoroughly trained and they're too seriously taken up with looking at cause and effect and tissue and fluid samples. There's a lot to be learned about the wasties. The doctors know this, but are determined not to say too much about anything that can't be trial-tested and backed up by empirical facts— which is to say they think they can find a cure. I appreciate that. There's a lot to be said about the facts. But getting too caught up in them is as crazy as looking for cures to everything. Sure, you want your Boeing engineer to know the facts. Every nut and bolt. And knowing those sorts of facts is what allows us to fly. But when you have the wasties you get a different impression of the world. You don't say things like "if every nut and bolt on this aircraft isn't just right the system will fail." When you have the wasties you don't even begin thinking like that, because it is accepted a priori that all systems are doomed to failure, and trying to make them perfect is as losing a proposition as the construction business in Babel. I would say, rather, "I wish I could never come down." So, while getting your facts right is nice and creates job opportunities, it doesn't mean that planes won't fall out of the sky. Thinking like this makes me horny. That's another thing about the wasties: you think of sex all the time. It's a little frustrating. One of the consequences of the wasties is you don't get to have sex because most people are repelled by you. It's not fear of contagion. They just don't want to get involved. So let's talk about airplanes because there's sex in them. I mean it. Not just in the machines themselves, but the consequences of unnatural flight. A person with the wasties, if he was in an airplane that was going down, would turn to his neighbor—even if that person was a perfect stranger—and kiss her. Just like that.

Because my case is fairly advanced, I would take it one step further. I would stand up and shout, "Okay, everybody! Start fucking!" And even though I know it's impossible to have sex in most passenger airplanes because of the seat belts and the tray tables, the idea is that at the moment of extreme mortal peril, every doomed organism within that cold hollow steel machine could be doing what all living organisms are meant to do above all else, i.e., reproduce themselves, even though there is absolutely no point in it and the extinction of the individual is the one and only certainty in all existence. Well, now you have a better idea of how a person with the wasties thinks of sex. That's the beauty of the wasties. You see the perfect beauty in all the despicable ironies of existence. It's a kind of acedia, an evil sadness that weighs you down. And there are no orgasms. That's the one thing I have to say I do miss from time to time. The feeling of release, the uncoiling of the spring of eternity, the discontinuity of being. It's not purely physical. Not at all. I would like nothing more than to go for days and days with a boner, a big honker of a thing. Of course, it's impossible because going outside would land me in jail. People with the wasties are many things, but they are not predatory perverts. They accept the fate of their nature in private. So, no, it's definitely not physical. It's organizational. It's getting everything all lined up that's the problem.

I don't remember when I got hit. Yes. The wasties hits you. POW! Like the flu or that fashion model named Fablio who was riding a roller coaster—surrounded even in that screaming contraption by adoring women—and POW a bird flew right into his face and splattered. Broke his nose! The picture was in the paper and all I can say is, if Fablio isn't well into the wasties now, he will be when he sees that picture of himself with bloody bird goo all over the shocked look on his face. Anyway, it hits you just like that. One day you're walking around doing everything the way you used to—which is to say blindfolded—and the next thing you know you've lost all power of speech and the familiar becomes suddenly alien and what was known becomes unfathomable and what was previously unfathomable seems strangely knowable. You are frozen in your tracks and prevented from speaking by a metastatic new knowledge that has no name. But never mind all that. I'm not asking to be believed. Just telling you what I have to say.

"You seem to be suffering from symptoms of depression," the doctors said early on.

Depression? That's like saying a dead person is merely suffering the consequences of mortality. The wasties makes depression look like a teenage kiss. It doesn't just involve the individual, the wasties involves all of us—and I'm not just talking about the Judeo-Christian Western world but human consciousness itself. There are no therapies and no excuses. Science is powerless. Religion is powerless. There is nothing that can be done—except nothing, and that's the beauty of it. Having the wasties is like being told not to think of the left eye of a camel.

There you have it.

My wife, Gina, found me. She found me from the beginning and she says she will probably keep discovering me anew day after day after day and that's probably bad because it's too late now. Too late for me, that is. I won't speak for Gina except selfishly, which is to say that I'd love it if she decided to become a nun. Gina and I go way back

back back and back again. We go back so far there was nothing but forward for us from the beginning. Now forward means a black hole. "Hold on a minute," Gina would say, "just wait right there." She doesn't put much faith in numbers. If our marriage has anything to do with anything, gravitational collapse is as good a way of putting it as, say, qualified non-dualism. Gina is great. Gina is pure. In the days before we had to pass notes, she was as good a listener as I was a talker and afterwards we'd go to bed and fuck each other to sleep.

But I'm getting way behind myself now. Or maybe ahead. I don't know. I seem to be starting where I wanted to finish, in some impossible someplace outside beginnings and endings when I became too contemptible to deserve as loving a partner as my wife, Gina. I have tried to let Gina in on my gratitude, but everything comes out sounding stranded somewhere between Petrarch and Rimbaud. Rimbaud had a fine case of the wasties. *Je finis par trouver sacré le désordre de mon esprit,* which translated into English means it was so fine he regarded it as sacred. It's why he quit his poems and went to Africa. Petrarch had the wasties, too; and was the first ever to keep records. He even recorded the day and time he got hit: April 6, 1327, at the first hour. I've tried explaining this again and again and Gina just gets this far-off, misty look in her eyes. She used to stroke my cheek with the back of her index and middle fingers until I began to suspect that she was seeing someone, and I cried and cried and carried on and told her to stop.

I have always loved Gina and will always love her and want nothing more than to continue to love her, except that in truth I no longer deserve her and so I can't. Love is not a prerogative for someone like me. Love, for me, is a recurring nightmare. It's what Goethe meant when he wrote *You have shattered the beautiful world with brazen fist. It falls, it is scattered.* In the days before the wasties I would have put it a little differently; but that was then and, like I said, something always gets lost in translation. Gina is like a recurring nightmare, too. When I think of her I think of all the bestial things she might be enjoying with men of another nature, men other than me, who are different from me and who, for all I know, are coming and going from her life like a motorcycle gang bang. Jealousy is not the word for it. I know I've lost her. The word for it is quicksand, the disappearance of the ground underneath your feet. And lest anyone think I'm merely feeling sorry for myself, let me say it is a marvelous thing to experience: to be drawn down into the earth. To become and be undone by your becoming.

I wish I could remember the night Gina and I first met. All I have is a vague memory of laughter. I believe we were laughing because what had been so urgently desired was so suddenly and noisily accomplished. Is that why our relationship was cemented so quickly? Not because we tore into each other but because we laughed afterwards. Orgasm is such a monumental anticlimax. You don't get very far if it's all you do together. You have to laugh, too. And cry and lose your patience and forget what brought you together in the first place because sex is too absurdly quaint a basis for growing old together, nothing more than affection passing between two beings plus the vigorous rubbing of body parts.

At around seven o'clock every morning I'd go into the kitchen where Gina was making coffee and we'd listen to National Public Radio. I used to read the newspapers back in the days when I could read. Now I just listen to the radio. When the radio is on, and sometimes even when it has been switched off, the radio voices swirl around in the atmosphere and mingle with the voices in my head. So just because I can't broadcast for myself, just because my motor is gone, my larynx is frozen, and I'm mute, well, it doesn't mean I'm not here. Does it?

Gina would butter a muffin for herself and for me and ask, "Sleep well?" To which I'd nod. She only asked yes or no questions at breakfast. When something requiring a more complex answer arose—which it very often did— she'd give me one of those looks that comes with no instructions, say "Never mind," and change the subject.

Our apartment was filled with every book and magazine and banged-up piece of furniture we'd ever acquired together. Acquired, I say; but I wish there were another way to describe the effort with which things seemed to accumulate around us. Procreation was definitely not involved, so there was nothing tender or sweet about the acres of stuff we acquired—that any two beings living together can acquire, for that matter. If matrimony and cohabitation can't guarantee happiness, it will at least give you things to shove out of the way at four o'clock in the morning when you're roaming lobster-like through your rooms and trying to fathom how it is that you and all the goddamned stuff managed to get here. In my pre-wasties days I was an English professor, so I had an excuse for all the books, though the having and the reading somehow got confused back there somewhere. They're still with me, though I can't remember if I've read any of them or not. I figure there's gravity enough in ownership, so go ahead ask me anything, anything at all!

"You've got to get out, learn to sign." Those were the words of Dr. Eremita who, referring to my old literary occupation, pointed out my Beckettish captivity—as if making reference to that Irish coxcomb turned Parisian prophet of glumness and antimatter is anything to invoke. I'll bet Beckett loved the Boeing 747. I can see him, tray table on his knees, jowls working through the tough chicken entrée, abandoning himself to the in-flight movie. There's a part in all of us that wants to eat the chicken entrée and watch the movie while, ears cocked, we listen in quiet terror for a stutter in the engines.

Sign language. That's what they call talking with your hands and face. The Plains Indians did it. It makes sense. Of course it does; and one day maybe I will go ahead and learn it. For now, the word suits me just fine. The written word, that is. *My* written words, since the reader/writer in me somehow got uncoupled and, write though I am able, I can't read the results and must live off the income from the semiotic blind trust my language has been placed into. At the very least, there's dignity in the way the written word reposes on the page; and it contributes just as well as oration does to the clearing of the seminal ducts (testimonial, from the Latin *testis,* which means witness) and prevents the unpleasant buildup of the steroid androgen testosterone (*testis* plus *sterol,* any of the group of naturally occurring steroid alcohols, plus the Greek feminine patronymic—*one*), which we all know is how most wars have started and why it's the men who go off and fight them. Believe me, it's all there: balls, alcohol and women.

So I can't talk. But I can still *testify,* by God! And that's just fine with Gina. She wants me to write, encourages me with all the infected inflections of a spouse concerned with an invalid's career. Write a book, she says, because in this day and age if you're not doing something to make a name for yourself your spouse considers you a waste of energy and begins to fuck around. Take that book I did write, the one they brought out in paperback which was called a milestone and which guaranteed me a job for life and a gravitas beyond my years. I can't even read, much less pronounce the title—partly out of embarrassment, but mainly because the milestone it represented was passed by and there have been so many intervening milestones that I'd need a global positioning satellite to find it.

"Can you hear me? Can you hear me?" Those were the first words I heard. Gina was standing gravely at my bedside and holding my hand. I could see her from out of the corner of my eye. There were tubes in my nose and everything was exactly as it should be when you've been temporarily rescued from your fate and placed in a purgatory of hope. She pressed a buzzer that summoned the doctors and nurses, who roused me from half-sleep into the full glare of my predicament.

Yes yes yes. I can hear you, I wanted to say. Loud and clear.

But I could not speak.

Of all that passed between Gina and me in those very first moments as we waited for medical science to come and explain, our brimming eyes were the means by which my permanent tenesmus was mutually acknowledged. There's no rhapsody more pathetic than the sound of a person straining and failing to speak. The image crowding my field of vision was of squatting, pants around my ankles, with all the forces of cubism and bureaucratic collectivism massing overhead and straining straining straining and only

11

managing to whelp a whimper or two, while inside this stranded English professor recited verses meant to calm and soothe and escalate the predicament into something transcendent. Robert Frost says *I have been one acquainted with the night*—but I have been one acquainted with *the wasties* and there are no nights blacker and no city lights more distant and there's a spill the most absorbent paper towel on the market can't wipe up, Robert Frost, though you probably had no use for paper towels in that honest New England captivity you remained so down to earth in.

"Let's go skating," she said one fine Sunday morning as we were eating breakfast and listening to a National Public Radio account of refugees somewhere, and behaving for all to see like a perfectly normal Manhattan couple at the turn of the millennium with a West End Avenue apartment and access to Zabars and the Internet and the stock market and frequent flyer miles. Did I mention that Gina is a lawyer and goes roller-blading regularly in helmet and knee pads and halter top and that she's fifteen years younger than I am and can't even be adjusted for inflation in 1967 dollars, whereas I can still remember getting buffalo head nickels in my candy money?

After a brief disquisition on why, exactly, going to the park to sit on a bench while she roller-bladed to the rhythms of boom boxes and roaming percussion ensembles (I love the sidewalks, I love to roller-blade, I love the traffic lights, I love the daffodils) would be good for me—meaning-ful pause, eyes bore straight into our circumstances—I mean, for *us*, I nodded yes. I wanted to say, "Yes, yes, yes by God! Let us go now, you and I." Just like old times. We used to roller-blade together—not because I'm the outgoing athletic type but because it made my seniority in years more palatable to her. I liked any excuse to go out with her, to roller blade, albeit at a more dignified, professorial canter than the all-out speed ballet derby that always left me far behind and flushed with amazement and good fortune to have a wife to love such as her.

So out we went.

And now I must try to remember, must try to narrate in the Heisenbergian haze, not merely how events were changed by my observations, but also by my participation in and recollection of them; and if that isn't enough to throw a giant shadow of uncertainty over everything I say, you'll at least have to admit to certain doubts—which is just another aspect of the wasties: You must doubt all experience and yet accept the consequences of it all the same. Imagine a ten-pound ball dropping on your toe and simultaneously joining Elvin Jones and McCoy Tyner in the rhythm section and not missing a beat! There are other words for it but they carry too many ritual connotations: people passing needles through their cheeks, standing for decades on one leg or extracting fruits and vegetables from various orifices. Or getting a haircut. Or going blind. It's all the same to me now.

So there I was. There I see myself. On a bench near the bandstand in Central Park. A sunny Saturday morning.

We got there readily enough, Gina beside me with her blades slung over her shoulder. It was unclear how far I'd make it, and at one point Gina stepped to the curb to hail a taxi. But I pulled her back. It wasn't necessary. I wanted to walk arm in arm into the park, as if everything were like it used to be. I no longer know exactly what I was thinking; but it probably had something to do with the distinction

between the present-at-hand and the ready-to-hand, and
the totality of the ontological possibility of Being-in-the-
Park, arm in arm with my beautiful, athletic wife, who was
talking cheerfully about a Tejano conjunto accordionist, a
woman named Antonietta from Mexico, who would be playing at the 92nd Street Y that night and reading from a new
collection of her poems. She was a friend of a friend and a
powerful and radiant human being who had overcome great
obstacles in her life. Gina wanted me to model myself after
her, perhaps later that very day. All this in the atmosphere
that hits you twenty to thirty feet into the park, of trees and
birds and dappled light and that gentle breeze that seems
always to blow across Central Park, except in mid-August
when it blows out of rooftop condensers.

Let me describe Gina once again. She looks like Sophia
Lollobrigida Welch, a Greco-Roman-Celtic beauty. She has
brown hair and long legs, but is also petite and birdlike and
has thick eyebrows that arch up high and full lips that she
never smears with lipstick and straight broad shoulders and
a broad back with an indent in the small of it and her
breasts are not too anything and her posture is earnest without being defiant and the words she chooses are always
accurate and appropriate without being forceful, conde-
scending, or mean, and when she listens a crease appears
between her eyes that caused me to love her before we had
even spoken.

We found a bench and she sat next to me and I watched
as she put on her blades and dug out the protective gear
from the backpack. I once bought her a Walkman but she
never used it. She said she preferred to move to the ambient
rhythms of the city. As I watched her preparing, I swelled up
with prosthetic pride; a stoic, special Olympics, but-for-this-

I'd-be-doing-that; like a seven-year-old kid watching the batter hit the ball out of the park and knowing, deep down inside, that he'd have done *exactly* the same thing.

Please indulge me. Allow me the sentiment of the portrait, accede to the melodious adagio of our Being-in-the-Park; take it for granted that Gina understood my predicament; take it as given that when she stood up, towering a good several inches above her normal shoe-shod height, and I glanced up at her from the bench bearing the look of dust blown from an open palm, she was moved to grief. Rather than pity, rather than strip me down to park bench indigence, she took me by my elbow and raised me to my feet and, bending slightly at the knee and balancing herself, perfectly at ease, she *kissed* me—not on the forehead but on the lips. "You just sit here and enjoy yourself. I'll be back in a little while." I dropped back onto the bench as she pirouetted, and with a mighty kick, glided away. I watched her disappear into the melee with all the human power I contained.

"By your policies they shall know you." That's more or less what the President said. By "they" he meant, not the citizenry, but all of posterity. It is by putting things in such grand relief that we come to comprehend our own actions. I understood that the President was speaking in terms of history; but the maxim is just as useful applied on the level of the man in the street, who must be known by his policies, too. It's fundamental. The owl of Minerva looking through the wrong end of the telescope.

I didn't realize he was the President when I first saw him. Ex-President, to be more exact. It happened while

Gina was off blading. If she hadn't just skated off and disappeared like that we wouldn't be going through half of what it is we're going through now. I'd be spared being called delusional and Gina would have had the chance not just to meet, but to shake hands with and get to know James Earl Carter, Jr., thirty-ninth President of the United States. He just walked up and sat down next to me and turned on that famous toothy smile and crossed his legs and rubbed what he called his "trick knee," in that genteel Georgian he speaks. I smiled and nodded along and listened. Ex-Presidents have to contend with astonished people all the time and so the fact that I didn't start babbling at him is probably why he felt comfortable. There was a man with him. Secret Service, I figured, by the fact that he kept a certain distance and wandered over to a grassy patch nearby and sat down as if it were the first break he'd had all day. We just sat there for a few minutes while President Carter massaged his knee and wiped the perspiration from his brow. I was watching him from the corner of my eye, expecting some sort of casual folksy comment that would set me at ease and indicate that he was just another mortal out in the park—something like "It certainly is pleasant out." Or maybe something rhetorical and touristy like "I know you don't eat grits up here, or biscuits and gravy, but I sure do like your lox and bagels."

But he didn't. Instead, he began to talk about the revolt against liberalism and the appropriation of agrarian populist rhetoric by neoconservatives and the far right and how it was used against him, especially after the malaise speech, and how voters, especially small farmers and workers, had been duped. I wanted to ask him if he was happy, if it was good being able to look back to his presidency and see it from a more distant perspective. But I couldn't, so I just sat there basking in the glow of the historical present, wondering what it was that had brought him to New York to go speed-walking in Central Park. People had begun to notice, and although the ex-President was very relaxed about the whole thing, I was getting nervous. One elderly couple walked right up to him and the woman said: "Mr. President, I want to thank you for everything you have done for our country. You are a shining example to all of us." Her husband nodded and a few people standing behind them broke out into applause. "Thank you. Thank you. You're very kind," the ex-President said and I wanted to tell him something to the same effect, and maybe even ask him to talk more about the malaise speech, because I had agreed with him at the time, and think what he said back then was probably even more applicable right now in the present. But I couldn't. I couldn't even get him to hang around and wait for Gina, because after the brave old lady broke the ice a crowd began to form in earnest and the Secret Service man got all agitated and officious and before anyone knew it, James Earl Carter, Jr., was gone and we were left in the shimmer and glow of his wake, which lingered for the entire time I sat there, only to be choked off when Gina returned.

It wasn't the shimmer that was choked but me. As we made our way out of the park, Gina winded from her balletic exertions and not so much talking as stating her pleasure in gasps of enthused speech, I could only wonder at the great wide gulf that separates James Earl Carter, Jr., from the likes of me, whose presence in the world is marked not by a shower of sparks and trails of light but by a stagnant, scummed-over pond.

My English-professor brain was sputtering madly and it

was pure agony until, at last, we got back home and I rushed immediately to the computer to bang out my response to the day's big event. While Gina showered I struggled to put into words everything that had transpired. I tried to cram it all into sentences and paragraphs; but it all came out ass backwards and wrong and though my fingers flew at the keys and produced yards and yards of prose, by the time Gina had come to look over my shoulder I had edited everything down to two pithy sentences: **I saw Jimmy Carter in the park. He talked to me**—and twisted around to see Gina's reaction. She was drying her hair, a towel wrapped tightly around her, exuding post-athletic calm and the smell of shampoo. She didn't look at me but kept her eyes fixed on the screen, as if unable or unsure of her response. To clarify, I added: **President Jimmy Carter!** Gina wrapped the towel on her head and put her hands on my shoulders. "That's amazing, honey," she said in a voice saturated with analytical thinking, and it wasn't the skepticism, but the way she began to gently squeeze my shoulder, is if to calm an overagitated child, that made me leap to my feet and turn upon her, red-faced, bursting with silence, and storm out of the room in a word-less rage.

Whereof we cannot speak, thereof we must be silent. Who am I, of all people, to argue with that? But what about this overheated room called consciousness, howling and groaning with tractate? I didn't want to start crying but I couldn't help it. When Gina came into the bedroom and saw me sitting there on the edge of the bed doubled over in a shame of tears, she couldn't help herself, either; and the two of us sat there for what could have been the rest of the day, bawling like stranded kittens. What did we do to deserve

18

this? The great unasked questions lingered between us as menacingly as masked and bloody-minded teenagers with access to guns and a liturgy of apocalypse. Goddamn! Can you believe it? We had found ourselves aboard a crashing airplane. Gaaahhh! Gina! You beautiful being! I am no longer me. I want to be you!

Gina wouldn't believe that I'd met Jimmy Carter in the park. All she would admit was that I'd been over-whelmed by some very comprehensive dream or hallucina-tion or even perhaps seen someone who resembled the ex-President. In her experience there just aren't enough atoms in the universe to account for such coincidences. "He's someplace in Africa monitoring elections. I heard it on the news."

That was supposed to settle the whole thing. She put it to me as we were lying in our bed listening to a car alarm down the street; and then she turned onto her side and said, "I don't know how to say this. I probably shouldn't say it at all."

I turned a look on her that said, say it anyway.

"You're not the same person I married."

For fuck's sake! I wanted to scream. I flipped on my IBM ThinkPad—which is a nice name for a troubling concept—and began to type out my response. Gina lay on her side, face lit by the glow of the screen. It was nearly 2 A.M. The car alarm clicked off at last and suddenly the only noise fill-ing the room was the rheumatoid clack of the keypad in my lap. I turned the screen and she propped herself up on an elbow to read it. I can't get that image out of my head. Gina's equipoise and the aquamarine light of liquid crystal glinting in her irises. It was the glint of our future, the unexplored frontier that we were doomed to a never-ending reconnaissance of.

She contemplated what I'd written for a moment or two, then settled back onto her pillow. I was about to type an addendum but she stopped me, swept my hand from the keys. "It's late. Let's go to sleep."

I put the machine away, lay on my back listening to the nothing that had crept up between us.

If you lie on your back long enough you begin to see the lineaments of every predicament, not just your own but of the entire world. You begin to discern every nuance of thought and speech on the horizon like volcanoes in the distance emptying themselves of ash; events and things which even the curvature of the earth can't keep from view, like the proposition that nothing is stable and yet definitions presuppose stable essences. Unless you are prepared to accept that all of life hinges on this and other wild conundrums you'll never be able to get past the gates of your wife's eyes or breach the levee of her heart.

The next morning we went back to the park to make me happy. No roller-blading this time, just a walk. Well, what passes for walking in my case, which is more like a spinning mass struggling to maintain an angular orientation minus all inertial coordinates and external torques, which the brain event had robbed me of, and which physical and occupational therapies are designed to restore. With Gina at my elbow all felt right, even the looks of passersby, whose glances in our direction used to dazzle and flatter me but which now had degenerated from admiration into gawking and spectacle: a furry and very pale man stealing through the streets of the world with a beautiful, ever-patient younger woman. She's not my nurse! I wanted to bark at every one of them. She's my wife! My partner for life! Through odium and old age, she with me and I with her— the sort of stable essence that makes definitions possible!

I had a hard time containing my enthusiasm, which was all but inexpressible anyway, except by a steady forward lurching and tugging at her arm. I couldn't wait to get back to the park, to introduce Gina to Jimmy Carter. Gina, Jimmy. Jimmy, Gina. I had no doubt he'd be there, if only as a favor to me. I'd lain awake all night remembering his speeches and the highs and lows of his presidency in such detail that I began to think I had been there when he got the bad news from Tehran; was at Camp David with Sadat and Begin as a sort of molecular presence diffused in the western Maryland air. Come to think of it, a small leap of imagination is all you need to participate in any world-historical event, past and present. The Conquest of Mexico, the Crusades, Captain Cook's voyages, the rape of Nanking. We are all there, past, present and accounted for, you and I and Eleanor of Aquitaine and Mahatma Gandhi—who would have liked flying the Boeing 747, I think, and probably is doing so right now somewhere, because passive resistance, when you think about it, is not all that different from piloting a jumbo jet, a tiny dhoti-clad man sitting in the cockpit on top of the horrendous momentum that makes intercontinental flight and the break-up of empires possible. Right?

With this and other distractions blaring in me, we arrived at the bench where Gina had left me the day before. I pulled her down next to me and we waited for James Earl Carter, Jr., thirty-ninth president of the United States. Gina had brought the *New York Times Book Review* with her.

Half an hour later she had finished it and wanted to leave. "Come on," she said, and rolled up the paper into a baton. "This is silly."

I shook my head. It was not silly. Sure, the ex-President is a busy man and has a complicated schedule, but I was certain that he would return. Gina sat back down and, after heaving a not-so-subtle sigh of frustration and hooking an errant bang behind an ear, took my hands in hers. Her eyes brimmed with tears. "I think we need to talk about making some sort of an arrangement." She let go of my hands, wiped a tear from her cheek. Oh how I loved her at that moment, and squeezed her hands with all the motor control in my being. "A nurse. Someone to help you get around a little better than I can."

That was all she said, but by her eyes I knew the words were a hastily arrived at concession to a deeper and more painful wish.

And so Mother Teresa came into my life.

Well, that's what I wanted to call her—as a joke, of course; because she didn't look one bit like that saintly old nun (who, come to think of it, would make an excellent 747 pilot, too since, when you think about it, nursing the dying and destitute is not all that different from transporting them across continents and oceans). I don't know how or where Gina found her, but a few days after being stood up by the ex-President, there she was!

When Gina brought her in to meet me I felt like some sort of family secret, some demented thing kept under lock and key. To diffuse the impression, I stood up and shambled over, trembling hand outstretched, mouth doing what for me must pass as a greeting and a smile. Thankfully, the pleased-to-meet-you gesture was fully understood, and since Mother Teresa—excuse me, Anna Theresa—had been fully briefed, everything went swell right from the start. The IBM ThinkPad was taken out and Gina and I showed Anna Theresa all our communication shortcuts—from the old fashioned, hand-pencilled note, to the word-processed macros that had been formatted with prompts and responses and could generate footnotes, indices, tables, outlines and humorous asides. I demonstrated by typing in the first message: **What is your name?**

"Anna Theresa," she said. "My friends just call me Theresa."

Gina beamed with delight, nervous spouse yielding to contended employer. Whatever they had discussed on the telephone prior to the meeting went unsaid and I followed with the next question: **Where are you from?**

"I am from Nicaragua. What is your name?"

I typed out my answer and Gina, seeing that things were off to a fabulous start, excused herself to make a telephone call.

Caruso.

She laughed and said, "Caruso? Professor Taylor?"

Caruso, just Caruso.

And off we were, Theresa and me, Caruso, the whole affair arranged by my own wife, Gina, who could now go out and do her thing and not worry or feel guilty for abandoning me.

I was happy to go along, more than happy, I was overjoyed. In that first period of time after coming home from the hospital all that seemed to matter to everyone around me was that I "get back to normal." Back is the operative word. Back back back to normal, which—the real being the rational and the rational being the real—is where the world is said to exist, and where I have been challenged to relocate myself. Naturally, I was terribly interested in getting back, too; and with such an urgency that I practically ran to all the therapies and couldn't wait to submit to and perform every test medical science had devised to return me to that blessed condition, where Idea and Concept are rolled into one like little Chinese boxes. All you have to do is *say* the word *normal* and everyone is tricked into assenting. Say: "All I want is to get back to normal," and the whole goddamned *world* will flock to help. They'll put themselves out, go to any length to get you there, back to normal—perpendicular, upright, vertical, made according to the carpenter's square.

Theresa set straight to work. Back back back we went. Back to the kitchen, the bathroom, to bed. Back to physical and occupational therapy. We backed everywhere together from 8:30 A.M. until 5 P.M. Gina was pleased to be going back, too. Back to work. Back to her regular schedule. Back to backing out. She was overjoyed to have introduced an organizing principle into the apartment, one that came in as she was about to leave and left shortly after she returned. There were no more groceries to get. No more waits at therapist's and doctor's offices. No more long-drawn-out idleness to ride out. No trials or tribulations except those which could be talked about in whispers among colleagues and friends. "She's got her hands full," I could hear them gossip. I heard the admiration; saw, felt, smelled it on her every time she returned home at the end of the day, and dropped her papers onto the kitchen table with a sigh of relief, while I, Caruso, lay in the next room dreaming of the New Man.

We were waiting for the downtown train, Theresa and I, heading to Washington Square Park for an afternoon loafabout. Gina had arranged it so she could work late and I could get out with Theresa and my rubber-tipped cane for some fresh-air excitement. A movie, too! Something called *Life Is Beautiful,* which Gina said would be something for us to go see together but she was too busy, so I should go with Theresa. Life is beautiful? A movie? Oh the blue light of the cinema, I wanted to say, tissue to my mouth, wiping away the gob of wisteria overhanging my lip. I could look at that blue light for hours, as I do pigeons on the window ledge or wisps of cloud passing over the city (which, when I look up, tends to keep me from drooling). And so there we were, the three of us, Theresa, me and my rubber-tipped cane on the platform waiting for the downtown train, and I hear a voice and turn to see Walt Whitman right behind us! Big floppy hat and beard, all hungry and dirty and bursting with joyful song and himself!

I touched Theresa's elbow. Look! Look! Look! I wanted to shout but could only gesture with my cane. It's Walt Whitman!

Theresa turned in the direction I was pointing. "Don't," she said and made to swat my quavering, outstretched cane as a cranky old lady growled "Hey! Watch it will you?"

There he was! Walt Whitman! Not crossing Brooklyn Ferry but waiting for the downtown train right there with all of us. I know everybody saw him because he was singing for all to hear. Flood tide below me! I see you face to face! And strumming a guitar, derelict and happy as all hours of the day—fifty years, a hundred years hence, ever so many hundred years hence!

I reached for Theresa and tugged her over to meet the bard; but she pulled away and said "Take it easy," in a nurse voice that she'd used once or twice on me before.

It's Walt Whitman! I wanted to holler, and since I couldn't, I wanted Theresa to holler it for me, to communicate it for all underground to hear. He was with us! Us! Men and women of ever so many generations hence! Just like he said he would be. I pushed my way toward him, Theresa half going with me and half pulling me back. Then the noise of the train and the rush of tunnel air and a surge of people on the platform and Theresa took some coins from her pocket and dropped them into the bard's out-stretched coffee can. "There. Come. Let's go." And we strained into the waiting train, me unable to keep to myself, yet incapable of anything else either. Walt Whitman! Right there! Out of hopeful green stuff woven.

People made way for us on the train, moved and slid and scooted aside, something which I had never experienced. There is definitely something about messy-mouthed men being escorted by young women—not groaning or moaning, but pop-eyed with silence and jittering with the forward motion of the train. As soon as we were seated, I yanked out my little notepad and scrawled: *That was Walt Whitman!*

Theresa read it, looked up at me and shook her head, tsk tsk tsk.

I was flabbergasted, nearly dashed pencil stub and pad to the floor but, checked myself, tucked it away and seethed instead. Why should she know Whitman? Is there a Nicaraguan Whitman? Is there? And rattling along underground I began to froth with the absurdity of the notion that literary expression runs in loose parallel across national cultural boundaries so that Goethe is a German Shakespeare, Charles Dickens an English Victor Hugo, Gustavo Adolfo Bécquer a Spanish Alfred Lord Tennyson—everybody traipsing around in costumes that don't fit and wearing garish makeup. I withdrew my notepad and pencil, surveyed the blank faces all around. Theresa sat next to me,

27

thigh to thigh, given over to my care, not merry, not grim, but moving along with the train and the clock.

I celebrate myself, and sing myself,
And what I assume you shall assume,
For every atom belonging to me as good belongs to you.

I put the notepad in her hand. She furrowed her brow to read, and I nearly melted when I saw the look of marvel in her eyes. Then her expression changed to the one of infinite sadness that adorns the face of every saint in every cathedral of Christendom.

I began to write, then stopped short. How to put this? It was too confusing. If I gave her dates she would only become suspicious. We'd have to start out all over again and far into the wasties though I was, I could foresee all too well where it would lead. So I wrote *Only in America,* and she nodded her agreement with a tsk tsk tsk, and a you-can-say-that-again, just as we arrived at Union Square and the doors opened. Suddenly I was on my feet. Come on!

"No!" she shook her head. "Not here," and she tried to pull me back but I was already out the door. "This isn't! Wait. No!" But I'd won, and was ruddering toward an exit.

We came up into the full glare of afternoon and she let me lead the way across Union Square, blinking and squinting and pointing to make her understand that I had an idea, an impulse, an inspiration. There could be no denying it and, behold, we entered the bookstore and there he was, staring down on the browsing masses from on high. Walt Whitman! Along with James Joyce and Virginia Woolf and Edgar Allan Poe, blown up and merchandised into banner-sized, decorative wall hangings by the retail designers at

Barney Noble's. I stopped short inside the front door, raised my cane. Theresa tried to swat it down but I waved and pointed, pointed and waved until a security guard stepped forward with a scowl and gave me no choice but to take out my pad. *That's Walt Whitman.* And Theresa looked up and she studied the poster for a moment longer and said, "I see what you mean. It's amazing. You're right, Caruso."

I was swollen with the pride of vindication as we left the store. Theresa's spirits had been buoyed, too. She began talking in a rapid-fire spanglish that I understood only partially, though the idiom streams inside my cabeza mixed with Alt Hochdeutsch, Latin, Greek, and Hebrew, a prodigious deception of lingual music that switches on and off all by itself like a radio in the next room.

We went to Washington Square, and Theresa sat us down facing the fountain, then moved us over to watch the chess players, and then one more time to watch the children on the playground. In all this time we remained in communication by a kind of telepathic mutual sympathy sustained by our vision of Whitman: Theresa, young, beautiful and poorly documented, biding her time as domestic nurse until her stars spangled and her American dream sprang to life; and me, cane clutched between my knees in a posture of outward decrepitude, but suffused inwardly with all the original energy of the Big Bang—each, in our own way, the best the world of our time had to show for itself, and the least it had to offer.

I took out my pad. *Have you ever been in love?* I read and reread the words, then tucked away the pad without passing it to Theresa. It didn't matter, after all. Knowledge like that was way beyond the needs and understanding of the moment. Whatever the condition of Theresa's heart, my learning of it could not have mattered to her. A short time later, I took the pad out once again and wrote *I am in love.* This time I handed the pad over.

Theresa smiled. "Your wife is very wonderful."

I took the pad back, nodding in agreement, then wrote *I am in love with you.*

Theresa said nothing but the corners of her mouth lifted in a subtle smile.

When did you come to America?

"When I was twenty-two."

How old are you now?

"Twenty-eight."

And now I had to return to my original question. *Have you ever been in love?*

Theresa smiled with all the good nature in her. "Yes," she said. Then, after a pause, "But I'm not sure if it was, you know, real. I always thought when you was really in love it couldn't go away."

And it did?

She shrugged. "I don't know. Anyway, I'm not in love right now if that's what you want to know."

It's none of my business.

She shrugged again, an ambiguous twinkle in the pupils of her eyes. "It's okay. I don't mind."

But I do. I do I do I do. And suddenly I could hardly bear to look at, never mind sit next to and be escorted around the city by her. At twenty-eight, still bobbing gently in safe harbor and protected from the open seas by her charms and her vanity. It was all I could do to keep my heart from beating out of my mouth, seeing in Theresa all the proof of youth's glorious urges, all contained, all drawn in and not yet burst and gone incontinent and berserk, but immanent and about to do all that. It made me think of Gina when we first met, everything about us that was innocent and immanent (though in keeping with the sociocultural economics of our advanced educations, also precocious and a little jaded). When we went out into the world in each other's company we were like a sovereign nation. I used to think that it took years to conquer territory that vast, but now I know it was conquered in a single night, and I know this not by how quickly the ground was taken, but by how quickly it was given back, sovereignty lost, transcendental unity dissolved into a splatter of nostalgia, orgasms, events and impressions.

I can't say how long we sat there. Wasties time doesn't move forward but is vertical. I'm sure it's terribly unhealthy from a cardiological perspective. Doctor Eremita and the rest of them prefer hysteria to take place on the outside, like atonality and serialism in music: chaos outside, arid order within. With me, I'm afraid, it's exactly the opposite: tranquil without, hysterical within. It's why people with the wasties make such good citizens.

Let's have pizza!

"Okay," Theresa said. We walked to Bleecker Street where Theresa found just the place and ordered for us. Two slices, two Pepsis. We ate at the counter. The pizza guy made eyes at Theresa. I didn't know whether to sit back and observe or insist that we go. He was big and ripe with unmastered vigor and muscles and black hair dusted white with flour. Finally, he said, "So where you from, sweetheart?"

Theresa ignored him but there was no doing that, not in his shop; and time passed until he asked "*Habla Español?*"

Theresa nodded, chewing, wiping the corner of her mouth with her wadded napkin.

"*Yo también!*" And as he slid a pizza out of the oven, flattened, spun and twirled a new wad of dough, he talked to Theresa as if they were inhabitants of a new world all their own. He had a thick gold chain around his neck, pearly white incisors, and all the power of Catholicism behind him, so talking cheerfully to a pretty young customer was natural and an easy thing for him to do. Following their conversation was not difficult and I quickly gathered that he lived in Queens and the pizza dough was nearly out and he hated running out because it wasn't his job to make sure enough dough was made the day before. They made their own dough, didn't buy it like the other places and that was important, the main thing. Theresa listened politely and kept dabbing at the corner of her mouth with her napkin, not coquettish but shy and well mannered, which was not lost on the pizza man. "She work for you?" He was addressing me, suddenly.

I nodded.

"She's a nice girl. You treat her nice!" This was said not as admonishment or out of some common interest but flirtatiously and as a way of paying an indirect compliment. I glanced over at Theresa, who smiled, not in the least offended, as Gina would have been by such a patronizing, sexist remark. In fact, I think she appreciated it and enjoyed what must have been the look of discomfort that came over me—not from fear or because I could not abide the man's machismo; but because I could see that Theresa was pleased by it and what do you say to a woman whose foreordained emancipation has not yet been achieved? Pizza for me has always been a casual affair. No wonder it is also the chosen repast of adolescent seduction. There's the Platonic circle-being element: round pie partaken of by splitting, creating yet more emptiness between, and sex the bridge that wedges us back into undifferentiated wholeness. No wonder the pizza man with his bulges and winks can wreak his effects! I watched for the batted eyelashes and the purring glances but Theresa did nothing like that, nothing even close, and for that I was grateful and also a little confused.

"You want another slice?"

I shook my head and Theresa shook hers too and put our grease-stained paper plates in the trash. He turned, indifferent, opened the oven and slid the big wooden paddle in and wrestled with two large pies as we made our way to the door.

"Wait a minute!" he shouted, gesturing for me to return to the counter. He was smiling, eyes alight with what was probably just one more of the day's many canceled chances. He beckoned me closer and I glanced back at Theresa waiting by the door and tottered toward the pizza man, leaning over my rubber-tipped cane with the careful exaggeration of a limp-necked aesthete. "You come back later and I make you a pie on the house," he exhaled, winking. "Okay, my friend?"

I backed away as he reached out and slapped my shoulder and broke into a hearty smile. "Don't forget. You come back, okay?" And he called to Theresa over my shoulder. "Make sure he don't forget, okay? Promise me!"

But half of the wasties is forgetting and the other half is despairing over what cannot be forgotten. Come back for pizza? How can you come back for free pizza when even the simplest of beings knows that despairing and forgetting are the two essential ingredients of a higher existence and, in the ever-unfolding immediate that is the canvas of experience, a free pizza can either be completely irrelevant or it can take on fearful proportions? If, for example, you look at the offer of free pizza as a man flaunting his goodness, then suddenly you find yourself trembling with the thought that the offering must not only go unaccepted but must also go unseen, because it lacks all humility and an Almighty and Just God can never accept an offering made in self-aggrandizement. So on the one hand, it's not free pizza that is being offered here, but a ritual catastrophe. Unless it's merely bait. To get the girl. And if so which is worse? Bait or self-aggrandizement before God? No mere differences these, but *the* differences, and the point is to annihilate as many such differences as you can in order to rise above them. That's Kierkegaard's word: *annihilate*. I prefer the word *forget* because there is less violence, a turning away from rather than blowing to bits. In any case, who said violent and furious intentions were necessary to the attainment of higher goals? That's exactly what I *mean* when I say the wasties is nothing less than the rejoined halves of forgetting and despairing.

So we left the spiritual wasteland of the pizza place even emptier with false promises of return, and walked down to the Anginika to see *Life Is Beautiful*.

And it was sold out.

Theresa was miffed. She blamed it on our detour for pizza. We examined the posters and show times for the other movies but Theresa had already seen some and the others held no interest. We dawdled outside the theater for a few minutes and I watched as Theresa flickered with polite helplessness. "Sold out," she repeated, but I couldn't see any sign that her irritation subsumed the larger and infinitely more pitiful predicament we had found ourselves in. I leaned on my cane, shrugged, and made no effort to point it out to her because I was fond of her and didn't want to shatter her innocence.

Let me describe her as we stood there on Houston Street outside the movie theater—black-haired, slightly but not too thick-waisted, coal-eyed, olive-skinned, with traces of whatever Indians slept with whatever Spaniards and remained on the land until the cities grew large enough to tempt them away. There was no society in the cast of her nose, and her eyes were clear and bright with the tinctures of belief and possibility. She had hard-knocks fortitude on her mother's side and unemployment on her father's, and it showed in the way she liked to dress: coquettish street sister of mercy. I don't know what she did after work, but would guess it had to do with both getting away from and wanting to have a family. She also told me she liked to dance, and now and then I'd imagine her in a skinny dress and cleavage, shaking her hips in Friday night frolic with bottle-strewn tables and cigarette smoke curling all around that has left no trace in her by Monday morning at nine o'clock when Gina has gone for the day and she comes back into my astringent life.

I don't know how long she'd been my boon companion aide-de-camp nurse and chaperone at this particular point. It could have been months or weeks. All I knew was Gina could not have been happier. Now we lay in bed together at night just like in pre-wasties time, Gina so returned to normal I began to think not only had the world suddenly become imbued with purpose but that the center, indeed, was holding. These were calm evenings, windows open to catch the night breezes. There were as yet no new revelations except the words of encouragement that came home from doctors and physical therapists written on chits of paper like notes sent home from teacher. Gina read each one with a look of funny concern and would ask me how I felt and look over my shoulder as I copied out my answer into the spiral notepad or pecked it out on the IBM ThinkPad. The circle seemed to have been knotted, and I began to wonder how long we would lie there undisturbed in bed together, side by side, content to accept our separate fates.

And I became frightened.

I was not ready to withdraw from life and love and marriage; yet Gina, it appeared, had already begun the retreat. Endowed as I was with late-twentieth-century enlightenment, the vision of Ecclesiastes began to cycle in my thoughts, and I saw our parallel repose not as a pillar, and what we had together not as a mutual possession, and I saw my mute, bedraggled self wandering from town to town, lodging wherever I found myself at nightfall.

A gallery! I pointed across Houston Street with my cane and pantomimed framed paintings, which caused a group of passersby to stop and admire my Chaplin-like gesticulations. Theresa took me firmly by the arm and marched me across the street. When we were safely across, I extracted myself from her grip and began to lead the way. In no time we found ourselves inside Leo Castrati Gallery staring at a perfectly bi-sectioned cow, two split halves encased in specially made tanks of formaldehyde, innards and outerds, open for all to see. It was more than Theresa could bear. She grimaced and said something in Spanish which I could not understand; and then, without the slightest glimmer of self-consciousness or beaux-art vanity, she said that this was not art but "bulgar chit" and insisted that we leave at once.

I pointed to the program to try and persuade her to reconsider. With my pencil stub I scrawled out a few sentences about Inner and Outer, the plastic arts and satire, mad cows and the political economy of carnivorous nation-states. But she was stubborn. Her eyes flashed with indignation, and as we were going out the door she said she had seen cows slaughtered for food and knew what hunger felt like, and was herself a refugee of war waged in the service of carnivorous nation-states. When we were outside she pointed at the building and said, "I am sorry Caruso, I am not *estúpido*."

We stumped up the block. I was bursting with pride and amazement at her sudden fierceness and halfway up the block sat down in a sort of mild protest on a delivery bay stoop and fanned my face with the gallery brochure. Theresa sat next to me. For a few minutes we watched the people walking past. Thoughts that were not my philosophy and philosophies that were not my thoughts pressed themselves upon my consciousness and I took out my pencil stub and made an attempt to draw Theresa into a discussion of contemporary aesthetic practice and *Dichtung und Denken*. Words like *thing* and *thinghood* came out, the sort of philosophy-speak that never captures the thing in itself but only distends our thinking toward it.

Theresa read politely. Then quietly, and with a quasi-confessional cast in her voice, told me that in her section on pediatrics, she had read about developmental language disorders, and that they most probably resulted from a perceptual dysfunction, and she was looking forward to getting certified as a pediatric nurse to help children overcome these and other obstacles.

My vision blackened. I had been set up! Theresa had been planted in my life because Gina believed I needed the special care of an as-yet-uncertified pediatric nurse? I felt my stomach go all empty and hollow. A gust of hot air blew a plastic bag into my lap. I swatted it away and watched it tumble off. Theresa, who Gina had described to me as a very pleasant young woman taking time off from school to earn a little extra money—was studying me for credits!

I flipped to a clean page in my notepad. *I am not a child!*

She patted me on the shoulder. "Of course not," she said. "Come. Let's go back home." She stood up, brushed the dust from her backside. "Come on," she repeated, and offered her hand.

I wanted to cry, shaken by a losing game and an image-world swarming with unfamiliar and mischievous shadows. I flicked my pencil stub into the street where it bounced with a plink, and was promptly run over by a car.

"Come," Theresa said. "Let's go." She proffered her hand. "Get up."

I didn't know what do; so I took her hand.

And bit it.

All I wanted was to prove my love for her, my commitment to improvement and the finishing of my animal nature. It's no small task in this unfinished universe we're thrown into day after month after year, where all is strange and where it is not good to be alone. It's the throwing part that is hardest to come to grips with; and I'm not talking sports metaphors, either—pitchers, balls and batters. It's more the violent trajectory of arrival, the landing on the doorstep with the vertiginous humming of time in your ears, the "Here I am! What's next?" It's amplified by the wasties, although everybody suffers it, and I don't know for certain but venture to think that it is worse for the poor souls who have been convinced by, and take pride in, the language of facts. The wasties switches those paths, rearranges language and facts, so that you don't come to think of yourself as an ego any more, but experience the world in the way sea grass does, an idle organism clinging to the floor, buffeted by the tides.

Sea grasses don't bite, of course. But that didn't matter to Theresa. She screamed like a Valkyrie and kicked me in the shins so hard I thought my legs were broken. A crowd gathered to watch as Theresa, standing several paces away squeezing her bitten hand, shouted abuses at me in Spanish while I, knees doubled up to my chest, rocked with agony. It wasn't long before we were being asked to explain ourselves to men wearing uniforms.

"You wanna tell me what happened?"

Through tears of pain, I shook my head.

The policeman took a step toward me and glanced over at his partner who had just begun his interrogation of Theresa. Full-grown men with canes don't let themselves go all to pieces publicly—not unless they're high, or nuts, or both. And, even if I had been able to respond, I doubt I could have satisfied him, because when crying overcomes a wasted person, it's nearly unstoppable, and everyone around becomes uneasy and deeply embarrassed because the face of grief is impossible to look upon without being drawn into the suffering.

The man's partner came over. "Don't bother," he said, "she says he can't talk." The both of them turned to look upon me, then walked back to talk to Theresa, who was also crying now and leaning against the building clutching her hand. She talked to the police for an eternity while I sat rubbing my eyes with the heel of my palm and enduring the idle stares of passersby. The police cast frequent glances in my direction as well, partly to make sure I didn't escape, but mainly for visual confirmation of what they were hearing from Theresa. It's like this in all nation-states. Visual surveillance is necessary because the repressive bureaucratic impulse is governed by the need to *see* and when it goes too far paranoia takes over and seeks to abolish the imagination. When imagination has been abolished, the real and the rational will always seem to coincide absolutely and make it is impossible for anyone to know the size and shape of their predicament, and you end up thinking you're living at the end of history. How it all works is one of the great mysteries of political philosophy, which means it will never be explained, although we do appreciate all attempts at the level of irony and can laugh in horror at the perversion of the *Obersturmbandführer* home for the holidays—but even *then* we have to admit that our laughter is only an imperfect expression of the derision the world deserves.

I looked at the sweat-stained backs of the policemen, belts hung with all the tools of control—sticks, guns, radios. Theresa was shaking her head—no no no. I wanted to go over and apologize but my pencil stub lay out in the street. Without it I was helpless.

I took my cane and slid off the platform, but hadn't gone two steps before one of the cops grabbed me by the arm. "Where do you think you're going, buddy?" And with one fluid superman heave he put me back on the old iron loading dock. "You just stay put until we decide what to do with you." He glared at me for a moment, then his features went all soft and he said, "Your nurse here says you got a problem. You want some friendly advice? Stay away from french fries. They'll kill you, dude. Not just fries, all processed food. Understand what I'm saying?"

I pointed to the pencil stub lying in the street but the cop ignored me. "You got your fats, see? Your polyunstaurated, your saturated. But it's the trans fats. Those'll kill you. They're in practically everything these days. Cookies, potato chips. You name it. You want to get better? Do yourself a favor and stay away from trans unsaturated fats. Can you say it? Say trans unsaturated fat."

Then he said, "How about partially hydrogenated vegetable oil. Can you say partially hydrogenated vegetable oil?"

He stood there for a moment, smiling at me like some grand figure of the public eye. "Never mind," he finally said. "I was just testing." And he walked back to join his partner and Theresa.

I gazed in helplessness at my pencil stub in the middle of the street and cried for my pencil—not just for my pencil but for all the poor lost pencils and the friendships that were lost with them. When you cry long and hard enough, you begin to realize that lost friendships are like lost pencils because both are necessary for communication, and when you lose a friend or a pencil you lose someone and something to communicate with. Of course, you don't communicate *with* a pencil! You use a pencil to communicate with; and if you think of a friend as a kind of pencil, an objective necessity, the means by which we inscribe our presence onto the world, make our impression—can you begin to see what I mean?

At last they stopped their talking and the three of them came to where I sat. Theresa stood behind the cops, still holding her hand and glaring at me from behind the wall of NYPD blue. "You got yourself one decent nurse, mister," one of the cops said. He was older and gone to flab with experience, whereas the young one with the aversion to french fries looked merely buffed and would only ever go to rust.

"She can still press charges if she wants," the young one broke in. "My advice to you my friend is be real nice to her, okay?"

The older one cut in, "Listen to me. This is what you're gonna do. You're gonna get in a cab and you're gonna go

42

straight home, right? And you're gonna stay there until you're fit to come outside and behave. You got that?"

I couldn't look at either of them anymore because they were clearly enjoying their power and had given themselves over to the pleasure of righteous admonishment and the disparagement of my dilapidated person. Theresa stood silently behind them, not exactly enjoying herself but clearly pleased by their reprimands.

"Your nurse here wants to take you home," the flabby one was saying. "You're lucky, mister. She takes her job seriously. I told her she didn't have to."

I looked up at Theresa. There were big tears in my eyes. I realized that I had thrown not just one, but all my pencils into the street—a whole box worth of them. And I sat there on that iron platform, enclosed in the formaldehyde of my own stupidity and on display like the vivisectioned cow of the artist's creation.

Theresa stepped between the two policemen and said, "Come on."

The flabby cop hailed a cab.

"You got money?" the younger one asked.

Theresa nodded her head. As a taxi pulled to the curb, the flabby cop said, "You ride up front," and opened the door for her.

"And remember to hold the fries, dude," the young one said. I crawled onto the rear seat clutching my cane for protection, and when the door slammed behind me I felt like a prisoner sealed up behind all my infamies.

Gina was home when Theresa returned me to her, nauseated by the cab ride. Had I had something to say for myself, I couldn't have said it, not after hearing Theresa tell Gina straight out, "*Señora*, I don't think this is going to work. Your husband needs psychiatric care, not a day nurse."

When Theresa showed the teeth marks on her hand, which had swelled and become tattooed with a deep purple bruise, Gina erupted: "Oh my God! He did that to you?" And she looked in horror on me, sitting humbled and confused on the sofa, staring at the tip of my cane. I could see that she was not equipped to know what to think; so rather than focus her attention on me, the perpetrator, she fussed over Theresa's wound, saying that she must go and see a doctor. Nurse Theresa insisted that it wasn't necessary, so Gina hauled her into the kitchen and prepared an ice pack.

I went to the bedroom and lay down. What else could I do? I had no version of events to offer and was certainly not going to dispute Theresa's. As I lay on my back and watched the motes of dust floating above me in the late afternoon shafts of light beaming across the Hudson, I began to thrill with anticipation of their judgment. A deep satisfaction overwhelmed my earlier sense of dread. My entire being was being scrutinized by the two most important people in my life. Two women! And me at the center of their concern! Count them—one, two fellow beings—fulfilling the absolute conditions of humanity and love by asking, "What do we do with him?"

Well, why not tie me down and suckle me? Just count those yummy breasts: one two three—goodness gracious! Four! That was one suggestion I might have made. Apart from the sheer joy of it, there is the pleasure of overturning emotional categories and social conditions—not an angry, impotent, frustrated, mean, dirty old man, but happy, contended, and narcissistic, full of appetites, and with a place permanently reserved in procreation.

Take me out to the woodshed and beat me, I might also have said. But, well, even if there had been a woodshed to go to, no woman I know of in life or in myth would have ever considered going there. Not even evil stepmothers, jealous stepsisters, ornery prime ministers, UN ambassadors or secretaries of state with arms negotiations and air wars on their résumés; not even the most bloody-minded Valkyrie among them would have chosen the woodshed, because it's dark and dank and women have their places reserved in procreation, too. Their nature requires light and the open air of truth; and even the nastiest, hate-filled woman never beats or smothers but abandons her infant on a hillside with a secret wish that it will be rescued and brought up by wild animals.

I fell asleep. I think I fell asleep. I can't say for certain because it's sometimes hard to know the difference between sleep and daytime consciousness, between an intuitive impression of what encloses you and an empirically oriented ontology of existence. Let's call it dreaming rather than sleep, a state that oscillates up and down the register of cognition too quickly for a coherent narrative to emerge, but strongly and jarringly enough to leave you with a pile of scattered images that come and go and come again, a vacillation of feeling-states that, like spinning blades of a fan, often seem to be reversing, moving backward—which is all I felt when I opened my eyes and saw Gina approaching the bed.

"You can't do this," she began with overly becalmed irritation. And then she flew into something that for even-tempered Gina must pass for a rage. She talked and talked and talked and didn't look at me, but just talked as if I were a passenger in a car she was driving and she couldn't take her eyes off the road. "I'm tired, Michael," she said over and over again. "Tired and worn out." And the gravity in her voice was such that I understood we were headed for the ditch whether she kept her eyes on the road or not. There was so little time. Her schedule was filled with so many reasons not to be with me.

I sat upright, feeling guilty. How was it that I was driving her away even as I wanted so desperately to keep her? Her anger had caused the crease on the bridge of her nose and the pits in her collarbone to seem deep and of great consequence. Her hair had just been cut, so there was an edge to it, too—razory, fresh, clean and in charge.

"You know you hurt her, don't you?" Her face went all dark with analytical thinking; and she just looked at me and her eyes grew cold and narrow because she was tired of dragging needs into our picture any longer. "Do you have any idea why?"

I could only fidget with the fringe of the bedspread.

"Do you have anything to say?"

I shook my head. A long silence ensued. It might have been a whole day, I don't know; but there was a buildup of CO_2 and I began to feel the pressure of rising greenhouse gasses in the room before Gina spoke again. "She's taking the rest of the week off. She isn't sure she wants to come back and wants time to think it over. There is one thing we both want, though, and that is that you start right away with a therapist. I've tried to support you and to respect your needs. But now it's time. I have the name of someone and I'm going to make an appointment." She had crossed her arms, and as I looked up at her from the bed it was as if I were observing the action of some provident totem, not being called to reason by an impatient spouse. The roller-blading had long gone out of my appreciation of her; and in the days weeks months since the wasties hit I had come to see her as so many new stars flickering in the distant heavens and I wanted to talk and touch and kiss and be loved by her *so badly.*

She looked me full in the eye. "It's time for you to stop feeling sorry for yourself. Time to start wanting to get better."

No no no no! I reached for the ThinkPad. It's time for me to start wanting to be a pirate!

She stood up. "I want you to think about what I just said." And she left the room before I could type Captain Kidd into the keypad or explain that, according to the statute, a pirate is *hostis humani generis,* a common enemy with whom neither faith nor oath is to be kept and that Cicero went even further in his definition by denying them even the name of "common enemy" since to do so would be to honor them with a status given to governments and states and thus allow them Solemnities of War and Rights of Legation—which, clearly, were not things that could be extended to pirates or people with the wasties who, like pirates, have no Commonwealth, nor Court, nor Treasury, nor Consent and Concord of the Citizens, nor some way of Peace and League. Some pirates (like Captain Kidd) were commissioned by the British Crown to go out and plunder and they were called privateers, which is a good name because it gets to the heart of their moral and legal predicament; and for those of us with the wasties it can be extended even further to encompass the grounds of our entire being. So, basically, if you think about it, pirates (and privateers) are radically rationalized proto-consumers, who know you only go round once in life so you gotta grab for all the gusto you can, and thus recognize that the vast difference betwixt Man and Man, the one wallowing in luxury, and the other in the most pinching Necessity, is owing only to Avarice and Ambition on the one Hand and a pusillanimous Subjugation on the other.

I had to reconsider my reasons for biting Theresa. Pusillanimous subjugation? Whatever the reasons, I have to admit, I can never hope to know them. If, by some miracle, I were given full access to the deepest recesses of my unconscious mind, I don't think I'll discover the reason there, either. The unconscious is not some sunken treasure chest that you dive down to, open up, and haul the contents up to the surface. Even if it were, and all you had to do was strap on the scuba and head for the deeps, there would be the problem of what to do with all that sudden wealth— especially when, in the harsh daylight, you discover that it's not all precious gems and gold coins, something you can trade with, but more like swampy, boggy real estate, something you're stuck with, something nobody else wants.

The best thing about muteness is that everybody asks simple yes/no questions. This is partly to save themselves the trouble of waiting for a more lengthy response, and partly because, deep down inside, they believe a person who can't speak can't think, either; and so they treat you like a tourist lost in their great big country and raise their voices as if you're deaf, and gesture with their hands and by exaggerated facial expressions, reveal more about themselves and their own turbid ignorance than you will ever show them of yours.

Dr. Victoria Eremita, my therapist, is an expert signer and no sooner had she ushered Gina and myself into the sanctum sanctorum of her office, than she began to explain why I might try to learn how to do it. Gina was in complete agreement. We made ourselves comfortable in the plush temple of her office and exchanged the perfunctory pleasantries, even went so far as to tell the doctor that my intransigence was the first obstacle she hoped I would be helped over as therapy proceeded. As if, I thought to myself, as if the entire problem is that I am merely unable to speak!

Dr. Eremita then assumed the quality of a bulb-studded mirror, switched herself on and explained that this first meeting was just to get acquainted and that Gina would be free to stay if she wished. Did she want to stay?

Gina looked at me for a signal. I nodded, and she settled back into her chair.

"Well, then, how about we begin? How are you feeling today?" She spoke in the manner of someone inviting you to fall to pieces. She was fiftyish, soft, big-boned, with white-blonde hair pulled back into a Danish and an open, pouting expression of indefatigable common sense in her face—a woman who, if she didn't have children had wanted them badly, and if she did, understood she didn't *need* them.

I glanced over at Gina, who was sitting like a witness waiting to testify. She was wearing her power lawyer clothes, carefully chosen to reinforce all stereotypes and clichés—which meant that she would be deposing some poor suspecting bystander later that very same day.

How am I *feeling*? Well, if a person with the wasties is anything, that person is an advocate of feelings too blatant and close for comfort, and stands like a flasher with trench coat wide open, not exposing himself to the mere looks of others, but also ameliorating the circumstances under which we all pass each other by without looking, as if blind and living in separate worlds. If the earth does not refuse to exhibit itself why should we, its creatures? Even if life is a continuous deception, it can't follow that one must hide from it. And even if it did follow, the only place you *could* hide would be on a busy street corner with your trench coat wide open, since what you are trying to hide from in the first place is the deception of the world; and the only way to do that is to expose yourself to it.

Right?

I turned on the ThinkPad, then put it aside and began to scribe my answer on the legal pad. *I bit Theresa.*

"Theresa?" The doctor asked.

"The day nurse," Gina offered. "She's partly why we're here. He bit her."

"I see," the doctor said. Then turned to me. "Why did you bite her?"

Gina swept her bangs from her brow and took up contemplation of the table edge. The room was silent except for the scratching of my pencil.

I'm not sure.

"You're not sure you bit Theresa? Or you're not sure you know *why* you bit her?"

Her parsing of my attempt at plain speaking had its intended effect.

Both. Maybe. And there's a whole lot more not to be certain of, too. Like whether what I want more than anything in the world is to have my penis return from its extended vacation to my brain which has been verging on the brink of ejaculation for some time now and which, if it remains in this tumescent, boner state for much longer might just come punching out of my forehead. If, by some chance, my sexual functioning should return and Gina and I were to fall back passionately into each other's libido—would I never bite again? I can't say, for certain. Was my violent act an expression of psycho-sexual frustration? I don't know. The whole world is collapsing all around me. I feel terribly ashamed of myself. If I could have it to do all over again—would I bite? Who knows? Maybe I would have kissed her instead.

I passed the sheet of paper across the table and Dr.

Eremita read it, her face betraying not the first glimmer of what might pass for a reaction. Gina seemed interested and she glanced nervously, as if she thought we were on the verge of something that would lead us all out of our predicament. When she had finished, the doctor put the paper aside, face down, on the table.

"Can I see it?" Gina asked.

A clinical look came across Eremita's face. "I'm sorry, but I have to consider what passes between a patient and myself strictly confidential. Of course, what your husband chooses to share with you afterwards is entirely up to him."

I could see a cloud of dislike pass over Gina and she lifted her briefcase onto her lap and stood up. "Then I will leave you to it," she said, putting her hand on my shoulder and squeezing gently.

"Please," Eremita said. "Don't be offended."

"Not at all. Not at all. I'm a lawyer. I understand."

"Thank you," was the doctor's final word. She led Gina out of the office and they conferred briefly by the door, but I could not hear what passed between them. Then, Gina poked her head back in. "I'll be back in an hour." She blew me a kiss which Eremita sidestepped with a jovial little skip, closing the office door with a brand of professional cheerfulness that can only be dispensed with a license. I had been doodling on the legal pad during all of this and Eremita left me to doodle for a minute or two as she arranged herself and charted the course of our relationship. "Is that for me?" she asked presently.

It wasn't. I stopped and flipped the page over to a clean sheet. She accepted the rebuttal with the utmost tact and pretended to dismiss it while plotting how to wrest it from me by crafty means. So I changed my mind—it didn't matter anyway—and flipped the page back and turned it so she could read:

There ain't no bugs on me. There ain't no bugs on me. There may be bugs on some of you mugs but there ain't no bugs on me.

She betrayed not the lightest glimmer of pretending to be amused.

It's a song.

"I see. Do you write songs?"

I nodded.

She sat back, crossed her legs and smiled as if I'd offered to buy her a beer she hadn't asked for, but would accept as consolation for my pathetic temerity. Were it not for the fact that a written record exists of my therapeutic exercises and that I created it myself with all the blind intention of an instinctual act, focused, singular, beautiful, and yet also just another in a world of similar objects—a spider spinning, say, or a beaver building—I doubt whether I would be able to recall anything that transpired. The delight that lies in psychotherapies comes from pretending to a world of self-evident meaning and yet also knowing that nothing is what it seems. There is license here, the freedom to utter impossible things while submitting to an authority that understands that the limits of language are the limits of the world and what you say is all you get.

I began crying. Eremita consoled me with a box of tissues and a sympathetic look; and when I explained that crying was my internal clock rising to the surface—not an alarm but an actual measuring device like those old German water clocks which count the minutes in tears flowing from the eyes of a nymph, in drops per minute, per hour, per day, until the reservoir dries up—that crying, for me—

for anyone with the wasties—is very much this sort of measuring thing, like cigarettes, a mechanism for counting down the end. Dr. Eremita smiled and said, "That is a very interesting idea, extremely interesting. But how does it make you *feel*?"

How do I feel when I'm crying?

She nodded.

How does anyone feel when they're crying?

She considered this; considered it for a good several seconds, then flipped over the sheet I'd first handed to her and, referring to it, asked, "Does it make you feel any *less* on the verge of ejaculation?" And she pointed to the paper before her. "Your words."

I understood what she was getting at. There was no good reason not to go there, except that I couldn't. The link she was making between crying and tears and ejaculation and the relief of sexual tension was too convenient, too much an analyst's way of formulating the world, for me to go padding dutifully along behind her. It also was just plain not so. Besides, I'd explained myself already; and that she could not accept my straightforward what-you-see-is-what-you-get explanation—angered me. Hadn't I said it clearly enough?

Theresa seemed more used to crying men than Gina because she was more plushly furnished with empathetic qualities and could appreciate the beauty of a weeping man, which is greatly nourished by a Latin bosom and thrives on invocations of blood, ancestry and dashed hope; whereas Gina, true to culture and conditioning, fretted and was concerned by crying. While she was familiar with and practiced tenderness and consolation, she also understood those things as palliatives and not as pageantry, as methods of bringing pain under control rather than as the ecstasy of a wounded heart. Where Gina would reach for tissues,

Theresa would rush to embrace, and if she never actually kissed my eyes, I felt it as though she had. In this iron country, a weeping man is as bothersome as one on a killing spree, and we condemn him for his lack of control and for disturbing the peace. Once again, I think of a crashing Boeing 747. Whether silence or hysteria reigns, it is the quality of the weeping inside that is the true human measure. Here! Run down the isles. Take your self-portrait. Are you straight-backed in your upright position, white-knuckled, compressed lips fighting tears dripping down your cheeks? Or rocking, beating your temples with your fists, and wailing for mercy? Or is that a smile on your face? Do you find something perfectly absurdly perfect at the way all your morbid fears have come to their fulfillment?

Theresa! Yes, she returned. As promised. Gina was standing by, ready to depart for work but also feeling the need to linger and observe as well as to thank Theresa for her big-hearted graciousness. "You don't know how grateful we are, Theresa," she gushed upon opening the door. Theresa politely waved away the gratitude, and marched straight across the room and into the kitchen where I was trying to eat cornflakes and listen to "Morning Edition" at the same time.

I pushed away my bowl of cereal. Theresa produced a sheet of paper, sat down at the table. "I have something for you," she said, and passed a piece of paper into my hands. I looked at it, turned it over once, then gave it back.

"You can't read it?"

I shook my head.

"But you can write?"

I shrugged, wiped the slop from my chin.

"Okay then, I read it to you." She stood up and leaned against the kitchen counter. Then she cleared her throat.

"Walt Wheatman. By Ruben Dario." Then she read to me about a grand old man who, serene and saintly, lived in an iron country and whose soul mirrored the infinite and who sang like a prophet and commanded sailors to row and eagles to fly and laborers to work and then went on his merry way with splendid imperial countenance. When she was finished she looked up at me. "Sorry for the translation," she said. "It is better in Espanish. You know Ruben Dario?"

I half nodded, half shrugged.

"In my country he is the most famous poet. Like Wheatman."

Gina was standing in the doorway, too curious to hold off any longer. "Can I see it?"

Theresa handed her the sheet of paper. I put my head down on the table, unable to hold it up anymore for sheer lack of honor. This caused Gina more confusion. After another minute of hastily expressed gratitude and what seemed suddenly to have become an almost sisterly consideration and general lifting of all barriers to a more perfect union, she hurried off to work.

I remained at the kitchen table, trying to understand Theresa on Ruben Dario's terms, but couldn't get beyond what I'd learned about Modernismo and had relegated to the attic in a box.

"In my country," she said, ending the long silence, "Ruben Dario is more famous than Walt Wheatman. I want to give you this poem because I don't like you to think I am *estúpido*."

She went to the sink and poured herself a glass of water, which she drank, filled, and drank again. "Have you been outside?"

I shook my head

"You look like it. Come. Let's go to the park."

You always leaf through the Great Catalog of Under-served Things from front to back. When it arrives the hardest challenge is *not* to throw it away. Who wants to have to look at what they can't have? Who wants to be reminded of what they do not deserve? On the way to the park I held on to Theresa like she was page one of the catalog, the one you come to after fanning through the whole thing, the one that presents itself with a plink of thumb and cardboard, the *one* page you have to look at and examine because it prompts the greatest wish and annihilates all chances of fulfillment at the same time. You stop there because you know inside your bones that you shall never have it—accidentally or essentially. All you will ever have is the desire.

Theresa smelled a little like pumpkin and when we got to the park the pungence changed ever so slightly and mingled with the smells of grass and leaves. It felt good to be walking so close to her nature like that, a gourd you scoop out whose essence is the shell, the form itself: proud, grand, supported by an exquisitely simple and clever architecture. I was a different fruit altogether, more like a lemon: bitter

57

rind and sour pulp you throw away after squeezing out the juice. The differences are best seen in terms of compost. The lemon is banal. You get a spiral of rind, mashed pulp, a splotch of juice. But the pumpkin is tragic; it is pure garbage, a vessel smashed, broken to bits, destroyed.

So we ambled along as lemon and pumpkin. We passed a group of Rastafarians sitting on a bench listening to music blaring from an elaborate contraption mounted onto a luggage carrier. Red and yellow and green with matted locks under knitted caps. I stopped to look and listen but Theresa tugged me away. It was useless resisting her, but I had seen enough to form an image of Rasta nature. It was a tamarind, bumpy and hardened shell with seeds that must fuse with other foods to yield their strange, synthetic flavor.

Then there was a man on a unicycle juggling flaming torches. A crowd clustered around, fat, green magnolia leaves around a huge open flower. He didn't fall or get hit in the head with one of his torches, but his fragility was there for all to see; and even as we all smiled and clapped at his skill, I could see him fluttering on the floor of his small-roomed apartment, being taken apart by someone—man or woman, I couldn't tell—who was bored with all his beauty and talent.

The farther into the park we got, the more I saw of fruit and vegetable nature. A deep well of gratitude opened up inside for the genius of Frederick Law Olmsted's vision, not just trees and rocks and water; snow, ice and blowing breezes—but man's handiwork, too: masonry and carpentry and constitutional government. A tall, thin carrot of a woman, as organic as anything cultivated by hand can be, came toward us pushing a stroller. You knew just by looking that she was destined to be julienned or grated and served

atop a bed of leafy greens more sumptuous to look at than ever actually to eat. And the raspberry in the stroller, all lumps and staining juices, an adored ornament that would go out of her life too soon to be of any real help in it. And there was a dog, too. Funny how a dog and its nature can never be parsed or parted. It was a retriever, and one look was all it took to tell that it was the true anchor of the entire family. Not the raspberry or the carrot or (and here I'm guessing, but I figured there was a banana involved—not purely as phallus, but more a nature that is concealed, which after peeling yields a mashable substance high in potassium and easy on the bowel).

Theresa was beginning to worry that I was getting tired. "Are you okay? Walking is good?"

I nodded vigorously. I hadn't walked so far in, well, not for a long time. We were crossing the Great Lawn and the sun was shining and the buildings rose majestically at the southern end of the park like cathedral bells ringing in my eyes. We passed a family of tomatoes on a large blanket, Beefeaters and Cherries, all ripe and red and soaking in the pleasures of the weather and carrying on without a care in the world. I would have enjoyed going home with them just to listen to their noisy enjoyment of life, which was self-contained and needed only strings to hold it all together. Somewhere in the middle of the lawn, Theresa decided it was time to rest and we sat in the grass.

May I see your hand?

She frowned but consented. My tooth marks were still visible, a yellowing purple wreath around the pad at the base of her thumb. She saw that I was smiling and yanked her hand away. "It's not funny!" she said crossly.

I nodded agreement. No, it wasn't funny. It was beautiful. Probably the most beautiful thing I'd done in all my life. I considered how to say so without offending her. The lawn began filling up with other food groups, grains particularly, hybrids and varietals; and following that, livestock and cattle. A whole socioeconomy began to form and I couldn't think of what to say or how to describe it to Theresa, so I just watched her taking in the scenery, saw how tremendous she was in herself, the fine dark line of her brow, the straight black hair, the corners of her mouth turned down. Nothing about her was deliberately shaped or adjusted but was graceful and *just so* without need of embellishment. A dog ran up and startled her, thrust a friendly wet nose in her face. She shoved it away as the owner trotted up, a merry eggplant who called the dog with a whistle and a twinkling smile that neutralized Theresa's irritation. I felt a flash of sexual desire. It was the gentle way she shoved the dog away, like an uninvited but not necessarily unwelcome advance. I struggled to ignore it, to shuck it off, by shifting my gaze to the furthest corner of the huge lawn. "You are getting red," Theresa said. "Everything is okay?"

I didn't want her to see me, so I nodded and tried to distract myself by watching a herd of sweating, grunting piglets chase a flying disk across a stretch of lawn.

"Ruben Dario was a big admirer of Walt Wheatman," I heard her say. "But I think he is making fun of him, too. You know? In the poem?"

I didn't think to answer, was trying to erase the flush from my face.

"Everything big and powerful must also be a little arrogant. That's what Dario is saying." She paused for a moment. "You surprised to hear me talk like this. You think because I come from a poor country, I am not educated."

I could not look at her for the red in my face and the uninvited phallus jutting from between my eyebrows. But I heard what she said and it reminded me of my seminar after seminar with the brave and pissed-off young, whose alertness to the imperial culture of aesthetic taste was so heightened as to have become painful and unendurable. I was about to agree with her and, by way of a taunt say, yes, not only uneducated, but dark-skinned and a *woman*—but the tooth marks in her hand already testified to my aggressive, imperialist nature, and since it is by our deeds that we are known, I decided to leave it at that. Let her see me for the horned, white male devil. It's much easier to live up to stereotype and makes for more fun over time as we do battle against them and overturn and overthrow everything we hate; so that when each comes crashing to the ground and the formal transition made from blind and ignorant and hate-filled, to insightful and brimming with compassion, unfolded out of the folds of each other, we are left with nothing more to do but go about our daily bread like sparrows.

"In my country I studied literature," she offered, attempting modesty but also thrilled to be capsizing me. "And I have read your book." Then she jumped up and held out her hand. "Come. Let's go."

At first, I thought she was trying to prevent further talk, forestalling, allowing time for the impact of her admission to be felt; but when I was on my feet and leaning on my cane, she pointed to the Shakespeare Theater and said. "I need to bisit the ladies."

The ladies? What ladies? We marched across the expanse of grass in the direction of the Theater, and I actually succeeded in keeping the pace for many yards before my right leg went all spastic and I had to stop and adjust for Doppler shift and admire Theresa, the only woman now on earth, a point in space where all moments intersected to fly off in all directions. She led me to a bench and told me to wait there for her.

Then something hit me in the head; not hard, just a light grazing that startled me.

"Sorry, dude! You okay?" A wild tuber approached me cautiously. "You alright?" He flashed a smile and bent to pick up the plastic disk that had landed at my feet. He was holding a lit cigarette. I scissored my fingers and without breaking stride he fished into the pockets of his jeans and produced a flattened pack of Marlboros. He handed me one; then, in consideration of the trouble, produced a second. "Need a light?" When I nodded he fished a packet of matches from the same pocket and tossed them to me. "Keep 'em," he said, and in one fluid motion he turned, hurled the Frisbee into the atmosphere and raced away trailing a red bandana from the rear pocket of his pants.

It took some effort, but I finally managed to light up and smoke half of the cigarette before Theresa returned. She was not happy.

"What's this? Caruso? Where you get that?" She snatched the cigarette and flung it into the grass. "You can't have cigarettes, Caruso! *Aye carumba!* I don't believe this. Where you get that? Someone give you a cigarette?"

I nodded, a mile-high nicotine smile spread from here to kingdom come. Theresa sat next to me, verging inexactly on tenderness, the way someone would sit down beside a favorite doll. "Listen to me, Caruso. This is berry bad. You can kill yourself. You understand? *Capito?*"

I tried to shrug my if-it-feels-good-do-it shrug, but she

wouldn't have any of it. "Smoking is bad, Caruso! You could die! I'm no kidding." When she said this her whole body shook with emphasis and her earrings jiggled and sparkled in the light. I noticed that her fingernails were painted. She had redone her makeup in the ladies' room, hinting at something planned for later, after she said good-bye to whatever will be will be.

I didn't rediscover the second flattened-out cigarette until the cab ride home. I was trying to peel a little strip of silver tape off the seat cover to stick onto the plexiglass partition. The sign from the city taxi commission was loose, and I tried to pull it off, too, but couldn't get my finger underneath it. Then I put my hand into the pocket of my jacket and presto! The cigarette.

When we got home I went straight into the kitchen. Gina was talking and talking and talking on the phone. She didn't see me, so much as see through me; and the nonchalance with which she said good-bye to Theresa and then called to me that she needed to make a few more calls made it all so much the better. I put the cigarette in my mouth, lit it and inhaled.

In a few moments Gina appeared in the doorway "What are you doing? Put that out right now." She marched across the room, and held out her hand. "Give me that."

I smiled the nicotine smile I had smiled at Theresa a short time earlier. I felt radiant, refreshed by gladness, as smoke lazed up from between my fingers in curls and wisps, exuded sweetness as it rushed from my lungs, blew past lips and nostrils and left me shuddering and longing to be filled up and my body distilled, heart valves yapping, bronchi swelling, tits and nipples and all my naked meat infused with the myth of heaven!

I put the cigarette again to my lips. She snatched it from me. "You can't do this!" she said and took it into the kitchen where she doused it in the sink. "Come on, Mike. Let's not be ridiculous. You know I can't let you smoke."

A little while later I was lying in bed. The light from the open door made a shadow of everything and I felt myself slipping deeper into the shade. I was on my back, staring straight up at the ceiling, watching how changes in atmospheric pressure showed up in cracks and bubbles in paint and plaster. I wondered if the spider webs in the corners of the room billowed gently because of these subtle changes, or if it was merely thermal convection. In the end I decided that a spider's beating heart caused its web to tremble because, even if it wasn't the scientific explanation, it had a ring of beauty, which is more important than truth.

Gina came into the room and turned on the light. I watched as she went to the closet, kicked off her shoes, scooped up a pile of dirty laundry and dumped it into the hamper. She began to undress and I tried not to look but couldn't help myself. How many times had we been here in this exact spot on earth undressing in front of each other? As purely unconscious and natural an act of cohabitation as there is; no Eros, no shame, no nothing but the simple act of undressing to go into the shower at the end of a tiring day. And talking and straightening up the room a little or, at least, moving things from here to there. She unbuttoned her blouse standing at the dresser, slid her arms from the sleeves, gave the garment a gentle shake and draped it over the back of a chair. When she reached back and unhooked her bra the scoops of her shoulder blades jutted and she did a little forward dip which released her breasts from their confinement and slipped the bra down her arms. The window! The curtains! I panicked, leaped across the room, nearly falling over the chair where she had just put her blouse.

"Hey!" she said as I grabbed the curtains and hurled them shut, nearly pulling them from the track they hung from. "What's the problem?"

When I pointed to the window she shook her head and laughed. "If anybody's watching, they've probably seen me a hundred times already. You never worried about open curtains before." She took off her skirt and laid it on the bed, she slid off her panties. I knew her so well, all her clefts and cracks, her crevices and chasms, her spots and wrinkles and ruts. I knew the exact geography of her beauty, every bit of it in proportion and in its place and acting pleasantly on itself: face neck shoulders breasts stomach pubis ass thighs calves feet toes. She was so beautiful, so very, very beautiful that I know not how I came of her or she of me, and I hated that I was gaping, and hated even more that I could only gape, and hate myself for gaping.

After she went into the shower, I went into the kitchen for a glass of water. I listened to the sound of the shower running. Gina and her body shared this apartment with me and my body. But what about our souls? Did they live here like our bodies did? In alternating states of dress and undress? Did they watch us as we ate and bathed and slept? Does soul love only soul, or can soul love body and body love soul? What is a higher form of love? I wonder why we aren't covered in fur like other animals? Furry mammals don't have these problems. They don't have to get all spiffed up to step outside and behave for all the world to see as if nothing sags, nothing stinks. They don't have to prove that the love they bear in their hearts is pure.

Gina came into the kitchen, put the tea kettle on and sat down at the table. She was wearing her crimson bathrobe, knotted tightly, hair slicked back. She was clean and fresh and ready to talk. "I know what you're thinking," she said.

You do? I sat up.

"I spoke to Dr. Eremita today." She paused, leaned back in her chair and fluffed her wet hair, smiling. Her eyes are blue blue blue, with large black pupils and with wet hair she looked like something precious put in a box a hundred years ago and taken out yesterday. She was Gina. My wife, Gina, the person I was supposed to know better than anyone in the whole world. She was sitting there, talking to me. And for a brief instant, everything familiar became strange. I did not recognize her or know who she was.

"Oh, honey! It's alright." She reached across the table and put her hand on my forearm. "Are you alright?"

I nodded because by then I had come to understand that, as long as Gina's hands were on me, I had to say yes to everything because if I said no she would remove her hands as if I were a stranger and, being a stranger, could not bring herself to touch me.

"I don't know what to say," she began slowly. "What can I say?" Her eyes began to tear and her nostrils were red and pumping as she spoke. I had to look away. Then she left the kitchen and went to lie down on the sofa. I heard the television click on, the flutter of channels changing; then the voice of the news, which filled the void.

After a short wait, I went into the living room. She glanced over at me, holding the television remote in her lap, feet propped onto the coffee table. I sat down in the chair I used to call my reading machine, but which now was more of a sleeping machine, and a place to deposit coats and bags and things. My glance shifted from TV to Gina to TV to Gina as she sank into the narcoleptic television-watching state. By the time the news was over and Ted Kippel announced that the theme of state funding for the arts would be the topic on *Mainline,* I was wide awake, she was fast asleep—and suddenly, it dawned on me that she was pregnant.

I lurched out of the chair and sat on the edge of the sofa where she was sleeping. Her eyes opened and I pointed to her belly. She took my hand and held it there. We stayed like that for most of the night, not talking, eyes mostly shut but popping open at times like risen dough. There was nothing to be said. Nothing. We just breathed and let our organisms filter the hours.

Theresa was amazed and could hardly believe it when I told her the next day. Gina was already gone when I woke up. Most of what there is to know about Gina can be summed up by her having left for work on time, and not having told Theresa a thing. Call it imperious dignity or shrewd, lawyerly reserve, a way of being in the world that always waits until questions are asked. Anyway, she had gone for the day and Theresa was reading the newspaper and eating a toasted bagel—which I nearly knocked out of her hand, shaking with impatience to get out the news.

Gina is pregnant.

Unable to utter the astonished No! that her eyes conveyed, she reared back, then pitched forward, then reared back again, while I kept up a vigorous nodding—yes yes yes it's true—and she leapt to her feet and I thought she was about to begin pacing, but she dismissed all thoughts of interrogation and tackled me in a South American lemur hug that had me gasping for air.

Then she pushed me back onto the cushions, put a hand on her hip. "How many months?" she demanded to know.

I fished pencil and pad from between the cushions, my diaper filling with glee. *37!!*

She took this in, nodding her head and making the obvious calculations. She regarded me with that all too familiar look of skepticism on her face, then yanked me to my feet and directed me back to the bedroom. "Get dressed," she said. "Quickly. You have wark to do."

Work? It never occurred to me to wonder what Theresa meant by "work." Getting dressed was work, and it took me twice the normal time because, as I was fumbling with shirt buttons and barely managing to tie my shoes, I envisioned a child struggling with the same labors. It made me smile to think of it, a little pot-bellied tot beating me in the race to dress, outpacing me down the hall to the elevator. I imagined a whole system of speechless communication developing between us based purely on mutual love and intuition, a private language known only to my child and myself. "Daddy says this. Daddy says that. I can tell what Daddy is saying just by looking at him." There was no face attached, no gender, no name, no personality except that of universal child. Sometime in the middle of that first night of impending fatherhood, as I lay there sleepless and uncertain, I realized that whatever the future held for me, there was now a tangible thread to my existence, out of the folds unfolded. And it was a pure gift.

I got dressed and off we went to physical therapy, the task of making me plumb again, plumb and in proportion and in tune with all the myths. Don't get me wrong. I wasn't against therapy. I understand that there is something heroic about getting on with an absurd and futile proposition. In that, I'm no different from all the other basket cases. I want to be a hero, too. More specifically, I want to stand aside and watch myself be made a hero, since a true hero is never aware of the heroic act and stands outside of all acts and actions.

Natalie, the therapist, always started with breathing exercises. She said that breath is where it all begins. It's called *prana* in Sanskrit, and when you say *ham-sa ham sa* as you breathe in and out over and over again you are calling on the inner swan, and when you continue to say it, and the words begin to run into and reverse themselves—*ham sa ham sa ham sa*—you are saying "this I this I this I" because *ham* in Sanskrit means "this" and *sa* means "I." So what you are really doing every time you breathe is saying *this I,* which translated from Eastern mystical into Western physical therapy means you aren't just straightening up to fly right, but calling upon your innermost flight attendant! So as I inhaled and exhaled, inhaled and exhaled, lying flat on the mat—*ham sa ham sa ham sa ham*—I became not just *this I* but the superbest man on earth, and not just a superhero, but a god unfolded out of the folds. And Gina was the goddess, the superbest woman on earth, the feminine primogenitor; and we were unfolded out of each other and still unfolding. I stood aside and watched my guts unfurl, all my organs and my brains. I could see everything in material creation as plain and beautiful and bloody as a visit to the butcher. It was not grotesque! No it was not. I watched and listened to each breath *ham sa ham sa ham sa ham* and it was not grotesque. It was delicate. Fine and delicate. Not: *Cover me, ye pines, ye cedars with innumerable boughs! Hide me where I may never see them more!* Not: *Hide the parts of each from other!* It was not grotesque or shameful and disgusting like the expulsion from Paradise. But just *ham sa ham sa ham sa ham.*

Tears began to stream from the corners of my eyes and run into my ears. And that was delicate, too.

"Is everything okay?" Natalie asked.

I nodded my head and she told me to sit up and helped me to cross and uncross my legs. Part of what I liked about physical therapy was that speech was superfluous. It was pure and simple: Do this. Do that. Try this. Try that. Followed by very good very good very good. It put me in mind of bats and balls and baggy-trousered fathers playing catch in the park.

I wanted Natalie to know. Why shouldn't she? For weeks she had been helping me manipulate myself back into some semblance of physical selfhood. Arms, legs, hands, feet— even mouth, by doing this silent yogic scream that she said helped my droopy facial muscles and might restore my old smile.

During our break I jotted down a note and passed it to her.

"That's wonderful!" She hugged me, and consulted the note one more time before asking the obvious question. "How many months?"

I wanted her to guess. My deepest machismo-starved erectile dysfunctioning self wanted her to see a virile man standing proudly before her, every archetype of male fertility and phallic power—not Wee Willie Winkie, but Bronze Age Man himself! She cast a discreet sidelong glance, which was meant to let me know that she had a hunch what I was getting at. What woman wouldn't? What woman doesn't understand all the sulci and fissures and occlusions of male sexuality better than men themselves do?

Just last night.

She furrowed her brow, bunched the sleeves of her sweatshirt up her forearm, glanced at her watch and said, "Time to get back to work."

But I was in the throes of counting back. In the glare of the fluorescent-lit, state-certified therapeutic environment filled with treadmills and StairMasters and a Nordic Track cross-country erectron! I was still waiting for her to guess. But she slipped by me with a hop, skip and a jump, back onto the padded part of the floor. By her eyes, I knew she would soon betray me, maybe even that very evening to a close friend over drinks. "God, it was weird. I mean, here's this guy who can't talk, or walk too well and . . . well, anyway, it was, like, he wanted to tell me he had just had sex with his wife!"

But she was wrong. Even with all her medical training and journal reading and sexual urbanity she didn't get it. I didn't want to tell her anything. I just wanted her to know I had just learned that Gina was pregnant. Let her infer the roaring good fuck we'd had for herself! Sure! What's so pathetic about that? God damn, I could have grabbed my spears and my armor right then and there and stalked off to fight the Trojan War, because the last thing I wanted to do just then was roll around a padded floor with my knees pulled up to my chest doing leg thrusts and listening to a certified physical therapist with one foot in yoga and the other in Columbia Presbyterian tell me what a terrific job I was doing!

It felt like the end of the world when our session ended. Even the options of whirlpool and little Dixie cups of orange juice—especially the Dixie cups—made it feel like some-how the human species had run out of breath and migrated into the anaerobic realm of pure consciousness where noth-ing happens, and everyone behaves professionally, like a German bath attendant handing out clean towels at Armageddon, taking cure after cure after cure until we've cured everything but despair, which manages to survive like a grand geological formation, neatly tucked into everything we see.

Comments? Complaints?

Evidently, Mister Lee was searching for answers and, to that end, had posted his e-mail address on the cash register. He put my bananas in a bag and dropped the Marlboros in on top of them. Theresa was waiting for me just outside, and it was all I could do to remove the little package without completely destroying the paper sack, and smuggle the little red and white box into my pocket before Theresa caught me. As I fumbled, I flashed a conspiratorial wink, something to let him know we were accomplices, in on this together. But Mister Lee seemed startled by the gesture and glanced away, frowning.

I remained there, half aware of needing something else and half trying to understand Mister Lee's sudden coldness. Then I pulled out my notepad and copied down the e-mail address posted on the back of the register. "You finish?" Mister Lee asked suddenly. Not, "Hurry up please, it's time" or "Good night, ladies, good night, sweet ladies"—poetic words of that nature; but just, "You finish?"

I didn't understand. I felt stung and suddenly in need. I wanted him to know that "You finish" was not a question, but a command. And on top of that, I was contemplating the purchase of one of those colorful and very handy disposable lighters on the display behind him. At the very least, I wanted his e-mail address so that I could correspond with him, address to him my comments and my complaints, perhaps even order up cigarettes for delivery. The sign outside his store did promise Free Delivery, after all.

"Caruso!" Theresa was standing in the entrance. "What you doing?" And before I could gain control of the situation, she had me by the elbow and was hustling me outside. She put the bananas into her carry-all bag while I clasped the little brick-shaped cigarette box in my coat pocket—edges clean and sharp, contents, all twenty of them, snugly packed together, speckled orange filter tips lined up neatly, side by side. Cigarettes.

Filtered cigarettes are like filtered light. By filtered I don't mean polarized. The transverse waves of light that come through the windows of my bedroom haven't been restricted in one direction in any way that *I'm* aware of. Maybe *diffusion* is a better word because it involves irregular surfaces and scattering and more closely resembles what comes to mind with cities and upright walking, sunlight beaming down onto streets and flashing off windows. The slopes of glaciers. Especially glaciers! I think about them every day, and usually first thing in the morning upon waking up, because there is something about glaciation that resembles the process of waking up from a deep sleep. The traces and tracks left behind in the transition from sleeping consciousness to waking consciousness are much like the tracks that glaciers leave in their wake as they move across continents and melt. You can see them on the backs of your eyelids and in Central Park, etched in granite boulders.

They were pointed out to me by John Muir, who thought them the most interesting feature in all Manhattan. He wasn't nearly as frightened by their imprecation of geologic time as he was by the hustle and bustle of the city. When I tried to show them to Theresa she was positively startled, not by the scratches themselves, but by the place where I had climbed to when I found them.

"Come back. Get down!" She shouted from below.

But I was too intent on the ascent, scrabbling up toward an outcropping. I had worked so hard to get there, abandoning my cane and moving forward hand over hand and on my knees. I could not have gone back down if I had wanted to.

"Go away," came a voice from above.

"Get out of here," came another.

They were both men, I was quick to notice; and even as they were shooing me away they were pulling up their pants. I tried to back down enough to give them their last few moments of privacy but I couldn't. My foot was lodged in a crack.

"What the fuck is wrong with you, buddy?"

"Leave!"

But I couldn't. So I smiled—or flashed my best approximation of a smile, which had the effect of scaring them; and suddenly they were scampering and scuttling away down the other side of the rock.

I tugged and pulled and tried to wrench but could not free my foot, so I lay face down and listened to Theresa's cries of exasperation and calls for help. When I looked up John Muir was standing over me—hands on hips, beard billowing in the breeze, without fuss or pickax, but simply six feet of lean, wilderness-hardened man with questioning eyes and thick socks and boots and a knot hole of a smile which opened up when he stooped down and asked, "Need a hand?"

With one mighty pull he hauled me up into the gully the lovers had just fled from. With a friendly wave he called, "It's alright. I've got him," down to Theresa who flapped her arms and called up a thank you. Muir motioned for her to walk around and up the other side. I lay back, exhausted, and watched as he ran his fingers over the surface of the rock, digging into crevices and cracks with his fingers. He began to collect samples, depositing them in some sort of bag, thoroughly engrossed in what he was doing. I would have liked for him to explain, but it was soon obvious to me that all explanation was unnecessary, that he was too exhilarated to speak, too captivated by the splendid pavement beneath our feet, the majestic lineaments of the ancient ice river that had carved its way through here, this very spot, millions upon millions of years ago. I wanted to ask him how long he had been traveling; if he was just passing through, or if he had been here for a while—winter summer autumn spring. I wanted to hear this old glacier pioneer tell me something, speak to me about his travels and his discoveries, even just a story about his dog or some acerbic, anti-civilization remark I could empathize with, like "I feel completely lost in the vast throngs of people, the noise of the streets, and the immense size of the buildings."

But he didn't. The only thing I heard him say came out sounding like "Goddamn condoms," but it could have been "Damn conundrum"—which amounts to the same thing when you stop to think about it because, even if you don't drag God into it, both conundrum and condom are there, a thin sheath that covers all of nature and prevents true intercourse, except in rare and accidental instances when the sheath breaks and some sort of meaningful, fruitful penetration is achieved.

I shifted a little to give him room to work. He glanced over his shoulder, then patted me on the knee and smiled as if to say "Don't worry my friend. We are all more or less sick. There is not a perfectly sane man in all New York," and went on collecting his specimens, which I was now able to watch him do from an upright position by leaning up against the rock. He had a long stick with a nail in it, some transcendentalist picking tool—homemade, for sure. I wondered if he had met or seen Whitman in his travels.

"There you are!" Theresa panted, stepping down into the little gully. She was flushed and cross and out of breath.

"You came up the hard way." John Muir smiled. "There's a path right over there." He pointed.

Theresa was not cheered or placated by this, and hardly seemed to have listened. She was pointing down the slope I had just ascended and shaking her head. "Your cane! You left your cane!"

Muir took all of this in and, without saying a word, he scrambled down to retrieve the cane. I leaned over so that I could watch his progress but Theresa pulled me back. "You want to kill yourself?"

No. I wanted to laugh. And maybe I did laugh; not from amusement over the alarm I'd caused, but from the new knowledge I had of Theresa. She was afraid of heights! Tee hee hee. By the time I had out pad and pencil, the cane had been returned. "I'd advise you to go that way," Muir said cheerfully, and with a wave he left to follow the streams of nature's laws and study their teachings and communions.

That was John Muir.

"Thanks God he was here," Theresa said. "I thought you was going to fall." She peered down the slope and drew back, shaking her head. "You make me crazy."

I pointed to the scratches and scrapes running in parallel across the boulders. I ran my hand over them, trembling with the power of the world they concealed, which was every bit as ferocious as the world of commerce and concrete and glass rising all around and yet grander for the spent processes they revealed. *They are glacier tracks.*

Theresa considered this as I traced the lines for her across the rocks, pointing to them with a shaky but steady enthusiasm. Glacier tracks!

Theresa contemplated them for a moment, then she took my arm and said, "Let's go." I followed down the path that Muir had so helpfully indicated, impressed as we went, not at how tame the way was, but at the number of buff men laying about and sunning themselves like battlefield dead. Theresa tugged at my arm. "Come on," she said. "I don't like it here. They are looking for sex."

Sex?

I stopped short and let go of Theresa, who tumbled forward and nearly lost her footing. The word acted on me like some sort of spell and a flood of images rushed into my head, not salacious or prurient in any way, but more like sequins adorning the pacific and harmonious joys of my unrequited urges.

"What are you stopping for?" Theresa asked. "Come. Let's go."

I wanted to tell her but could not have succeeded in words. I glanced about, seeing not only the glacier's tracks but the glacier itself, its chambered hollows dripping and trickling with icy water in curling, swirling, channels and, simultaneously, the warm lusting bodies lazing about the terminal moraine of the park, not separate, but united across aeons of time. A chorus began, and I could see beyond the chambered hollows of glacial ice into the chambered buildings surrounding the park, and beyond them into the chambers of every beating heart. A roar of joy rose upward upward upward, in harmony with the traffic in the street, and spread outward outward outward into the dimmest reaches of the cosmos. I looked at Theresa, who with hand outstretched, was beckoning for me to follow, and I thought, why not fuck in the park? Why not fuck *only* in the park? Just as I began to dig into my pocket for pad and pencil so that I could post this question to Theresa, a man brushed past, nearly knocking me over. He held a pair of binoculars to his eyes and was pointing up into the trees. "A pileated woodpecker!" he called, and stopped beside Theresa, binoculars still trained into the canopy.

He was grey-haired, neatly goateed, and dressed in conspicuously weathered cotton leather canvas outdoor gear. "See it?" he asked; and then, in a good sportsmanlike gesture, offered the binoculars to Theresa. "Up there!" He pointed. "*Ceophloeus pileatus abieticola.* Northern pileated woodpecker. The first I've seen here in the park. The very first."

Theresa accepted the binoculars with a shrug, and followed his pointing finger to the object of his fascination. She listened as he explained that the bird was a forest dweller and very timid, that it eats insects and berries and acorns and is generally resident where it is found, which meant that there would likely be a nest someplace in the park, which he would very much like to locate. He said it was highly unusual that such a bird would choose this busy park for a place to live and how extremely lucky they were to spot it. Theresa nodded and returned the binoculars to the man, who looked through them for a moment and then, smiling with satisfaction, offered me a turn. When he realized he was dealing with an invalid, his eyes beamed with Good Samaritanism, and he actually put the strap over my head himself and put his hand on my shoulder to steady and help me train the glasses with gentle nudges. And then I saw it! A very big bird, all fluffed with feathers and that special urban indignation that comes from feeling trapped, like when the subway doors slide shut before you are fully off the train—Hey! Just a goddamn minute here!

Do woodpeckers fuck in the park?

"See him?" the man kept asking.

I nodded, which caused me to lose sight of the bird, and suddenly I was disoriented and no longer looking into the canopy but through the trees and across the park at people going about their privacy. Theresa said, "Give them back."

"Here, I'll take them now," the man said.

But I was entranced, and held tightly onto them. A woman was sitting alone on a bench eating a sandwich and brushing the crumbs from her lap. She was every bit as fascinating as a bird in the trees and wore a weary lunchtime look and chewed deliberately and sadly and not on her own time but someone else's. I could not help but think that for such a person a good fuck in the park would have ten times the restorative effect of a sandwich, and as the man gently coaxed his binoculars from me, and Theresa apologized on my behalf, I tried to think of a way to tie up all my discoveries, but nothing would cohere.

I retreated to a bench and fell backward onto it, dropping my cane at my feet. It hurt. Theresa and woodpecker man glanced over at me and then resumed their conversation, snippets of which I managed to decipher. Their talk veered into a description of some research in Costa Rica and the American Museum of Natural History, which was indicated by a westerly wave of the binoculars. "Are you a scientist?" Theresa wanted to know. "An ornithologist, actually," he said, and produced a card, which Theresa accepted with thanks and promises that caused me to rise up from my seat in protest, not just over the man's gesture but over all the city's extravagances, each and every one of which I felt piling into my way, and which I can only describe in terms of my mother's grocery store chitchat and the pats on the head I was forced to endure while my real concerns ran rampant and unheeded and game after game was played without me.

Suddenly, and without warning, they broke off the conversation and the man ambled over and sat down on the bench next to me. I looked to Theresa, who smiled and nodded her head as if to say, "Yes. He's the real thing. A gentleman of New York." But there was too much unbridled eagerness in her for me to assent to the perception. Gentleman of New York, indeed! I know a patronizing old lecher when I see one; and especially one trying to pretend most people and himself are alike.

"I understand you are interested in glaciers."

The words sent a chill up my spine and I tried to move away. Sure enough, he began to melt all over me. He indicated the rock formation I had just come down from, and began to tell me about it. By now, Theresa had sat down on the bench, too; and I felt myself outflanked and outmaneuvered—on the one side by a blatant expression of lechery, and on the other by an assertion of agape and compassion, each of which needed me to get at the other, but neither of which had any use for me beyond the moment.

"You showed me the tracks," Theresa interjected, less on my behalf than on behalf of a womanhood comprehending her finiteness and seeking accommodation for it. "He climbed up there, scared half the death out of me."

Woodpecker man twisted to look. "Is that right?" he exclaimed, and pressed the binoculars into the orbits of his eyes for an ostensible look. I couldn't help but notice the severely trimmed goatee and how it altered the definition of his jaw line and seemed intended to inspire misjudgment and poor calculation in anyone inclined to profess an interest in the man behind it. The greyness of it only deepened my suspicion, and brought images to mind of opulent bathrooms with marble-topped counters and luxurious fixtures and countless garters unbuttoned and unhooked, not in weariness or mindful of approaching death, but in denial of all those things by a lifetime subscription to the ideology of youth and all the necessary magazines.

I pushed away from him, as far and as hard as I could, sliding across the bench against Theresa, who grunted in surprise. "Hey! What are you doing?" She shoved against me with both hands. The man took the binoculars from his eyes and trained an uncomprehending look upon the both of us that was meant to signal his unfazed amusement. Then he stood up. "I'm sorry," he said. "I didn't mean to crowd you."

Theresa stood up. "Please. My apology. Caruso! You are being rude." And her apologies carried them a few steps away where they resumed talking in Spanish, smiling and nodding as if each had chanced upon the next phase of the other's life. After a while the man said, "You have my card. Feel free to come by the museum. I'll show you some pileat-eds close up."

"Thank you," Theresa said, and she offered her hand, which the man seemed grateful for the opportunity to shake, and as he did, he looked at me and frowned with feigned concern. "Feel better," he commanded and with a final pump of Theresa's hand, bid adios and was gone.

It wasn't until we were at Starducks and she had her latte in front of her that Theresa spoke to me again. When she did, it was all James Bond and woodpeckers. Then she tugged out the card. "Look here, Caruso. Look at this." She flashed the card at me and read, "James Bond. Curator of Birds."

Maybe I wasn't interested in birds and maybe I was. In any case, it didn't matter. I was not about to let James Bond, whoever he was, become a lethal factor in my existence.

I took out my pad.

He is looking for sex.

"You pig!" Theresa erupted. She tore the sheet from the pad, crumpled it into a ball and threw it at me.

Like everything else in the park.

This time I held the pad out of reach. She read, blowing steam from her cup, and didn't answer except to grunt and shake her head. I wanted to explain that I found nothing wrong with sex in the park, per se; that there was something sublime and beautiful about sex in the park, and I didn't mean to sentimentalize or make more of it than what it could be—a basic fact of existence, nothing less. I certainly didn't mean anything kitschy by it, no orgy conducted out in the open—Snow White and the Seven Dwarfs with fertility rites and sound track included. What is Snow White but an allegory of thwarted male desire, anyway? Droopy, Dopey, Happy, Sneezy, Grumpy, Sleepy and Doc— all prevented from fucking Snow White because the very element of their nature that defines them also makes them repugnant to her. Especially Happy! Good God! Can you imagine?

It was time to call for a moratorium on walks in the park. There had to be another way of enjoying the mellowness of the seasons and green landscapes, ducks, squirrels—even pileated woodpeckers—without exposing Theresa to the depredations of men, who if they weren't chasing birds and pretending themselves into pastoral idylls with technical language and snappy outdoor gear, were hunting women to put in their nocturnes. Why birds, anyway? Why not tigers?

From now on no more going to the park.

Theresa blew more steam from her latte. "Why not?"

It's dangerous.

She laughed, and held on to her cup with both hands. "What else am I going to do with you?"

She did have a point, but need she state it so . . . plainly?

"We're lucky to have the park to go to. It's the perfect place for us."

Suddenly, that Boeing feeling came over me and I watched Theresa calmly sipping her coffee and merrily refuting me. A roar of jet engines overtook my hearing. I felt a sudden drop in air pressure and a falling away of direct intuition and of the sources of everyday experience, and we flew into a cloud bank, masses and towers billowing overhead, underneath, all around.

"Are you alright?" I heard Theresa ask over the static crackle of the intercom. "You want to go?"

Go? Go where? Where was there to go to?

When we got home from Starducks everything was quiet. Theresa left me to my distractions and went to the kitchen to prepare our lunch. My shoes never came off easily enough in those days. Socks were even harder. I don't know why, but it probably had to do with the linkages and dynamics in my newly administered bodily physics. In therapy you learn all these handy little ways to circumvent your condition, a sort of anti-law that emancipates you from the restrictions of your disability. It's mental trickery, mostly. You have to imagine things on both micro- and macroscopic level and oscillate freely between them to get anything done. I can visualize "bring knee to chest," or "rest chest on knees," but it won't get me very far until I conjure my likeness and my shadow, and dredge up a cacophony of word-images from the buried mansion of the forgotten me. And then, lo and behold, beneath thy look O Maternal, with these and else and with his own strong hands the hero harvests—a shoe! And drops it to the floor and repeats the process—but never exactly, because I'm no steam-powered harvesting machine but a man trying to get off his shoes; and the next time around it goes knee to chest, and I ask, by handless hints do conjurers rule? Do mannikins forbid the soul? And lo, the shoe drops and, for an instant, *I* rule, conjurer and soulful mannikin both, sitting there on the chair just inside the door, listening to Theresa setting out the soup and sandwiches.

And then came the knock on the door. It startled me because it sounded like the echo of my shoe dropping, but with enough of a delay for me to wonder if the apartment had grown so huge and the echoing walls so distant that sounds now took seconds to bounce across it. Theresa appeared in the kitchen door, then crossed the room, wiping her damp hands on her apron, all domestic and cozy, as if expecting a visitor. I lunged, tried to block her from reaching the door. Don't answer! Stop! But instead of springing between Theresa and the door, I fell off the chair with a thud as she opened it and let Mr. Langer into my life.

Straitlaced, he stated his name, extended his hand to Theresa and asked if he could come in. "I hope I'm not coming at a bad time."

Theresa helped me to my feet. Langer moved further into my home, greedily taking in what he could of my life with glances all around. "I was told that now might be a good time to stop by," he explained to Theresa, who led me to the sofa where I sat down to regain what dignity was left to me. "I tried calling but you must have been out."

"We are about to have lunch," Theresa began.

"Don't worry. I'll only be a minute. I wanted to introduce myself." And, as if invading the existence of another were the most natural thing to do, he sat himself in a chair, hitching up his pants with a bankerly pinch at the knees, and looked me squarely in the face. "How are you feeling today?" he asked.

I took as full a measure of the man as I could but grew confused because I knew who he was and yet also had no clue. There was ice in him, in the steel blue of his eyes and the grey white mop of hair that seemed both stiff and lank and wet and dry and his own and not his own at all. His lips were a tad too moist and a shade too red to be a man's, and yet his face was freshly shaven and there was a little cut on his adam's apple that bobbed above his collar and marked him out as one of the fastidious and totally unscrupulous members of the sex. They always go hand in hand— unscrupulousness and fastidiousness, the inner man seeking to disguise himself. The situation is slightly altered with the wasties, where the inner man remains hidden and the outer man bare-assed and not so much in need of a disguise as simple, sensible clothes without difficult snaps or buttons. A speck of fat or flab might have made him seem less dangerous and severe; but he was trim and narrow and smelled just enough of lotions to let me know that he had come to me for one purpose and one purpose only—to cut short my bliss.

I looked past him to Theresa, who was standing in the door to the kitchen with a look of distracted patience that made me feel suddenly bolder. I sensed that she didn't like the uninvited visitor any more than I did; and though she couldn't throw him out, she clearly wished he would leave so we could get back to our noon routine.

Langer assumed a frighteningly serious expression. He cleared his throat and sat forward. I felt every degree of his ice and my burden seemed suddenly colder and heavier because I didn't want him to think I was a sissy. I wanted to kick his ass! But something stopped me at the last minute. It was a lucky thing, too, because once the violence in me gets started it takes a call to SAC Headquarters and those guys in Cheyenne Mountain to deter me before I go thermonuclear.

"I think you better go now," Theresa interrupted.

Mr. Langer stood up. "Of course. I only meant to introduce myself." He stood there over me while I wiped the juices from my face. Then he stepped quickly to the door, saying things to Theresa that were not meant for me to hear, and left.

"Don't worry, Caruso," Theresa told me later, as I tried to spoon soup into my mouth. "Nobody can do anything to you. Don't worry. My uncle Oscar says, no matter what, a family is a family and nobody has to worry as long as they have a family."

I dribbled and didn't have a clue what she meant, but let the words soothe me like the soup we were eating. I didn't understand Uncle Oscar because I didn't understand family as a mode of protection but one of predilection, something to *have*—which, in the end, is all you can hope for in hedonism. Theresa wasn't clued into any of this, of course; and as much as I felt it was my responsibility to let her know how much life outside social contracts differs from existence within them, and how obligations for the wasted have nothing to do with the throes of duty or faithfulness to a great idea, I could not bring myself to interrupt her faith in things, and listened passively as she changed the subject and talked about a house this Oscar was buying and the mortgage he had applied for. Her eyes shone as she described it all; first the house, which was someplace in New Yersey and had a garden and hardwood floors that needed refinishing and rooms for everyone including herself, which would be in the basement that needed finishing but that was no problem because Oscar had a friend who was a contractor and he would do the work. "So, Caruso. I'm moving to New Yersey!"

I nodded congratulations and would have liked to kiss her right on the spires of the dreams that had brought her to America, which dreams for the wasted only provoke the sort of world-weary condescension that brings dissipated civilizations to their end.

"Oscar will talk to Mrs. Taylor about the forms."

Forms?

"To show the bank I work for you. They need all the informations."

Informations?

"To get the mortgage! You understand?"

I nodded my head but had no idea what she meant
except that *mort* means death, and a *gage* is a pledge o
challenge to fight, and that whatever it was Theresa and
uncle Oscar were up to sounded extremely dangerous.

"I will rent the basement from my uncle. I'm movin;
New Yersey, Caruso. Over there!" And she pointed in
general direction of New Yersey but I didn't bother to t
around.

"Oh Caruso! You don't know what am I saying,"
groaned. But it wasn't true! I did know what she was sa;
Better than she knew herself. I knew very well all the r
lations she was in for.

The phone rang and she answered with *"Bueno?"*
immediately grew apprehensive. "Jes. He did. No. N
good. Only a few minutes. I don't think so. No. Jes. N
Correcto. I don't know. Here, you tell him."

I held the phone to my ear and heard Gina's ag
voice. "Michael? Are you there? Listen. I'll be home
hour. Did you get that? I meant to tell you that Mr. I
was going to stop by. I'm sorry. I just completely forgo
from CarePartners. We can talk about it later. Can y
Theresa back on for me? See you in an hour."

Then, everything seemed alright again. I went ii
bedroom and turned on the radio and listened to a
sion about Middle East peace negotiations, the metr
report (Holland and Lincoln Tunnels, fifteen-minut
accident westbound on the George Washington
West Side Highway slow from the Boat Basin to 42nc
and I began to understand why I was afraid of clowr

When Theresa came in to get me, I was about {
cent dressed, thirty percent made-up, and jiggling
under the rapture of my new understanding.

"Caruso! What have you done to your face? A*y carumba!* What's going on here?" She snatched the lipstick from me and picked up the mascara bottle and the rouge. "You're making a mess. Look at this!" She gathered the rest of the makeup equipment and took it into the bathroom. I followed her, watched as she sorted all the little bottles and phials and tubes. "Look at you!" She tugged me in front of the mirror and we stood there for a moment appraising my handiwork.

My face was beautiful, a cross between Schiele and Soutine—Schiele from the waist down, with dangling, jiggling, useless dick; and Soutine from the neck up, all reds and ochers and crimson and blue with heavy black pencil lines and inscrutable, manic sadness. A clown! A useless, helpless adult, someone to scare and make children laugh—and not with hedonistic pleasure, either, but in triple-decker horror of the full-scale predicament.

I began to laugh, or what passes for laughter with a bungled larynx, and reached for a lipstick called The Eternal Wound—a French thing that must have cost an arm and a leg; but Theresa slapped my hand away and turned away from me. "My God, Caruso! Go and put on your pants!"

I looked down at myself, holding on to the edge of the sink for support. Theresa squeezed past me and out of the bathroom. I followed her but she headed straight into the kitchen without looking back. "*Pantalones,* Caruso! Don't you come near me like that. I want you dressed!"

When I returned to the kitchen, Theresa was looking out the window, averting her eyes. "Clean your face," she said without turning around. The words had the edge of will and not wish, and came from someplace far outside both of us, and were spoken with pure aim and split-second timing, so that I would have no choice but to obey.

But I was not eager to relinquish sovereignty over myself so easily. So I wrote a note and passed it to Theresa over her shoulder.

I want to be a clown.

She read it and passed it back over her shoulder without turning around. "You are not a clone," she said, then turned and marched past me straight into the bathroom. I heard the faucet and a moment later she was back and holding a wet washcloth out to me. "Here," she said. "Wash your face."

I shook my head and sat down—not Soutine meets Schiele anymore, or even Marcel Marceau or Emmett Kelly, but a king without a country, a man destined never to please. She put the washcloth on the table and sat down. "Let me tell you a story," she said. "Can you listen?"

I didn't nod or shake my head or look at her, but kept my eyes on the washcloth steaming on the table. My left leg began to bounce and "Yankee Doodle" began to play some-where in the far reaches of my hearing and I listened as she told me about her uncle Oscar, who was a school teacher in Esquipulas and after the Sandinista revolution was sent to a little village called Muy Muy to teach the peasants to read. He was gone for six months and while he was away his wife had an affair with a local playboy named Roberto which the whole town soon learned about because Roberto went around bragging about it. Anyway, Roberto disappeared one day and everybody said he had gone off and joined the Con-tras and when Oscar returned from Muy Muy everybody in the town expected the worst. They waited and waited, but Oscar went back to teaching at the school and acted as if nothing had happened. People asked how things were at home with his wife and he never said anything except that everything was fine and he was happy to be back. Finally, his neighbor told him about his wife's affair, and said it was an outrage, and that the whole town knew about the affair with the Contra. Oscar should do something to defend his honor. But Oscar just went about his business as usual and did nothing and nothing happened. Then Oscar's wife got pregnant and everybody said the baby had to be someone else's because they had been married for five years and she had never become pregnant, and it could only mean that not only was Oscar not a man, he was a fool because he allowed himself to be cuckolded and humiliated. Everyone in the whole town told jokes about Oscar and one day a boy at school even called his wife a *puta* and Oscar took the boy outside and didn't hit him or even punish him but just talked to him outside the classroom so everybody could hear and after that people made a joke of trying to provoke Oscar the school teacher. But he was never provoked. They had a little boy and called him Jesus and from all outward appearances they were a close-knit and happy little family.

"Now what do you think?" she asked when she had finished. "Is Oscar a *payaso*? How you say? A clone?"

I didn't know and could not have answered her if I had. Clowns aren't born, they're made. With the wasties you live like a clown, or a king without a country. There are no possibilities open to you, no tasks left to do. Nobody expects anything from you and you expect nothing from yourself. Yes, Oscar is a clown.

Theresa looked at my note and shook her head sadly. "No. You are wrong Caruso. Oscar is not a *payaso*! He has self-respect! All the people laughed at him. But they could not make him a clone! Never!" As she said this she picked up the washcloth and began to wipe my face with it. She rinsed and wiped and rinsed and wiped until my skin felt raw and all traces of Expressionism and Emmett Kelly were gone and we were all alone again, *inter et inter,* between and between.

"So tell me," Gina asked, when she got home, "Did you like Mr. Langer? He wanted to meet you before we took things any further. It's important that you feel comfortable."

Comfortable? Comfortable with what? We watched each other for a long, long time. If Gina said anything else I didn't hear it. As a matter of fact, I didn't see anything, either—except that she had colored her hair a deep, Bedouin henna. Somehow this slight transformation in her looks, combined with the swelling belly, the Being-In-The-Beginning-Of-Being-Made inside her, the contact with something unseen, began to frighten me.

"What's the matter? Are you alright?"

All I could do was stare dumbly at her because I didn't know. Finally, after fumbling with pen, paper, I was able to ask Who is Mr. Langer?

"I want you to think of him as a friend." Those were her words and that's what she said. Naturally, all the proper male hormonal nuances were lent to the phrase "friend" and it was all I could do to get myself up out of the chair and out of the kitchen into my room—Gina calling, "Hey! What's the matter? Come back!"—where I threw myself onto the bed. A short time later I felt Gina's hand on my shoulders. "It's alright, honey. Please. Don't be upset. We'll talk about it when you're ready," and she massaged my shoulders gently and for what seemed a very long time.

When I woke up it was still dark. I was on my back, taking in the silence, and snippets of conversations I wish I had had. The trouble with conversations you wish you had had is that they can never become actual conversations because life can't be revisited or revised, and wished-for conversations must remain the partner-less affairs of children in their beds and people standing at tombs.

Falling in love was the only way out. It came to me all at once, and not in the context of an actual conversation, but in the context of all the partner-less talks and wished-for conversations I have ever conducted. Falling in love. Of course! It was exactly the weapon I needed! Just the thing to protect me from the misery of knowing that my wife wanted to get rid of me, and might probably perhaps even be sleeping with the entire male population of New York City. I sat up in bed, took in what I could of the surrounding room, at once familiar and unfamiliar, here and not here, now and never. Of course, merely declaring my love for another woman would not fix anything. But it would sure as knowing when to shit make me feel better. If only Theresa had been my therapist instead of my nurse. I would have preferred her to be the object of my love; but with the wasties, judgment always stands aloof from appetite, and thus my offenses could only amount to errors of the mind and not the blood. On top of all this, the demands of the master/slave dialectic are such that I was left with no other choice but to go with the buxom, bun-scratching Dane.

I went to my desk and scribbled out the words which I hoped would startle Gina back into love with me. *I love Doctor Eremita*—and I would have added, "So there!" But with the wasties you have to stand vigilant guard against overstatement, so I didn't.

"Well," was Gina's initial response. "I guess I don't know

what to say." She had changed into her bathrobe, an immodesty that never failed to inspire secret hopes in me. National Public Radio was in the middle of a story about nuclear smuggling, which seemed too important not to listen to and, next to which, my own pathetic importuning was trivial. Yet Gina did grow thoughtful as she took in both my wounded fancy and the news of yet another country that was now thought to have most of the necessary ingredients for a nuclear device. "Have you talked to her about your feelings?" She sat there, stirring her chamomile tea. It wasn't puzzlement in her eyes, but something more complex and incomplete. A flash of satisfaction welled up inside when I realized that her attention had been diverted from nuclear proliferation and was now focused entirely on me.

"I don't know much about it," she started out, bearing a gentle, thoughtful expression I had not seen in ages, but which instantly reduced me to tears. She handed me a tissue from the sleeve of her robe and continued. "Transference, I think they call it. I suppose it's a good thing. It means you're making progress." She smiled the sweetest smile, put her hand on my arm as if offering up an oblation, and there was nothing Baghdad, P'yŏngyang or Beijing could do in the world that could have compared with the thrill of appeasement that raced through me. "Now, about the man from CarePartners. I'd like to take you to see Knickerbocker Estates tomorrow. I've hired a driver." With her hand on my arm all I could do was stare at her and wonder where she ended and I began. Knickerbocker Estates? Weren't we there already? Stepping nimbly as matadors among Manhattan's plunging traffic? The longer I sat there and tried to take it all in, the less I wanted to know of Knickerbocker Estates; and then, slowly, that meerschaum,

Niew Amsterdam somewhere up the Hudson became the central axis of all my dread, and I was overwhelmed by a terror of being buried above ground.

"It's a great place," Gina continued. "Not too far away. An old estate. Beautiful setting, nice staff. When I went there and saw it I *knew* it was just the right place. I should have said something to you earlier. But I didn't want to bring it up until I was absolutely sure about it. I want this to be *our* decision, honey. I want what's best for all of us."

And she patted her belly and began to cry.

I began to collect Marlboro boxes and stack them in a corner with the tops facing out. MARLBORO. It wasn't on aesthetic grounds that I planned to wall myself in with empty boxes, though they do look like little bricks and I'm sure there are fine-tuned sensibilities out there who would get something out of such an assemblage beyond the obvious allusions to Poe's "Cask of Amontillado," Joseph Cornell, Andy Warhol, and a witty answer to Willard Van Orman Quine's ontic question: What is there? (Have a smoke!) Nope. Nothing of the sort. All I wanted was to measure how much time we had left together.

As soon as I had come up with the plan, I wanted to explain it to Gina. She was at the kitchen table working on some legal brief. She was not exactly forthcoming in conversation anymore. What was there to talk about? The weather? The birthmark on her inner thigh? The radiance of the aurora borealis, which had begun appearing in the sky at night?

I handed over my calculations:

$$(16 \times 8) + (15 \times 8) \times 2 = 496$$
$$496 \times 12 = 5952$$
$$5952/3 = 1984$$
$$1984 \times 20 = 39,080$$

"What's this?" She looked at the paper in her hand, then at me, then at the paper.

I pointed to the last figure, 39,080, and laid a single Marlboro box on the table, hoping she'd make the connection between it and the number of cigarettes I needed to smoke in order to have enough boxes to wall myself in with. Until I put an exact number to it, I don't think she had ever considered the teleological dimension of smoking. It was something I had only recently discovered myself. At any rate, a number was what I now had. There were plenty of things to consider. For instance, at exactly what point would the door become blocked? I would have to calculate this and other things down to the last cigarette, meal and glass of water.

Planning and calculation are necessary for everything in life, and when you have the wasties the calculations must be exact to the last decimal place. I spent great stretches of time looking out the window or simply lying in bed. There is something about looking out windows or lying on one's back that both invites repose and startles us into a higher experience of our existence. I'd go to the window late and sometimes I would swear it was broad daylight outside, what with the glare of the moon and aurora borealis and the effulgent afterglow of the sleeping city. I tried to get myself outside from time to time for cigarettes or just to see how far I could get, tap tap tapping with my cane. But, inevitably, I'd be overcome by the surrounding topography, the lawlessness of the wild, and be forced to return to my room to wait out the rest of time.

"Where did you get the cigarettes?" Gina asked. "Did you go out and get them yourself?" And I was reduced to having won the spelling bee because I'd made "progress," and even though "progress" involved reviving a smelly old habit—at least, well, I had gone out on my *own,* which implied a whole host of other actions, like getting dressed and finding the right amount of money and taking the elevator and walking down the block and going into the shop and asking, well not asking, but indicating what it is I wanted and paying and counting the change and then finding my way back to the right building and getting the elevator again and pushing the right button and getting off at the right floor and finding the right apartment and having the key, opening the door and locking it behind me and, having forgotten to get matches, using the burner on the stove to light up.

She picked up the red Marlboro package, turned it over in her palm as if unable to decide what it represented. Then she put it aside and sat down, ready to talk. I loved Gina when she sat down to talk. She had a special look she put on and it was easy to get carried away in her presence. I always ended up wanting to say more and wishing I had said less. It was exactly the opposite when she spoke: I wanted her to say less while wishing she would say more. Then her nose began to redden and her eyes began to brim. "I don't know. Sometimes, I don't know. Sometimes, I just feel like . . ." She wiped the tears away with the heel of her hand, tapped the cigarette box idly on the table. "It's like everything was just yanked away from us. I don't know how else to say it. But that's what I feel." She shifted her gaze to the far end of the room. "I had a talk with Dr. Eremita the other day. Did I tell you she called? You know what she said? It's all still there, she said. It's all still there. Do you realize how much that little statement means to me? I think about it everyday. Everyday. It's all still there." Her gaze shifted from the cigarette box in her hand back to me. "Do you mind me talking like this?"

I shook my head.

"Good. Because I need to talk." Her eyes began to well up again. "If you only knew how much I want you to get better. So we can go back to . . . sorry, I mean go forward. Forward! Oh God, I don't know." She swept the cigarette box from the table and buried her face in her palms. "I don't know I don't know I don't know."

A short time later, I was sitting there with a glass of lemonade and the Tweety and Sylvester crazy straw that Gina gave me as a present, a practical thing that not only makes drinking easy but fun! Gina was fixing bean burritos and having seltzer with lime, which was her favorite drink and part of a larger coping strategy that included rollerblading, her substitute for wings—not the feathery soft kind but the hard, swept-back, man-made 747 kind that require enormous forward thrust and propulsion for flight and intricate circuits and hydraulic controls, everything riveted together, and precarious, and as thrilling as a half-empty bottle on a slow afternoon. It felt like she loved me. Just to make sure, I put on NPR which, as I've said, is how I situate myself in world-time—not by events, but by the familiar voices that are the anemic but no less reassuring foreground of the news.

All was calm. I watched as she rolled the tortillas with black beans and chopped tomato, avocado, cilantro and onion, folding and slicing it all neatly into manageable bite-sized pieces. She topped off my lemonade, poured another seltzer, sat down across from me and, just as I began to eat, she pushed her plate away and looked at me with a fearful tenderness. Her features hardened up a little and she said, "I don't think I can take care of you like this anymore." Before I could swallow what I had just put into my mouth she was on her feet, pacing the short length of the kitchen. "Don't misunderstand. It's just that. It's just. Can you understand?"

I wanted to nod but instead I shook my head. It wasn't that I couldn't understand; but I saw no reason to profess an understanding, the consequences of which were uncertain. I couldn't get the food down, so I let it fall from my mouth onto the plate and bent forward, sipped lemonade through the Tweety and Sylvester straw, feeling every bit *hostis humani generis*, plopped down into Gina's world of self-evident meaning, and not once but twice removed from my own, where nothing is what it seems. Which was fictional and timeless? Which was temporal and real? I could not have said. Nobody can. But I would have gladly forfeited either for a strong draught of fresh air and a stroll in the park. Gina knew she had unleashed something strong into the atmosphere, and for the next few minutes we retreated into the enough-said portion of her monologue, the part where in the old days I would have chimed in with a version of things not too different but just dissimilar enough for the necessary illusion of synthesis to propel the conversation forward. But instead, I concentrated on Sylvester chasing Tweety, and the lemonade spiraling up the plastic straw, and the sour taste exploding in my mouth, and the awkward, painful sublimation that goes with having nothing in focus and everything before you. Gina was leaning against the counter, clutching her glass and keeping silent council. I tore a sheet from my notepad, drew an arrow and pointed it to her untouched plate of food. Eat! And with a look of resignation, she returned to the table and began to eat like someone performing an unpleasant kindness. She didn't finish, either; but wiped her mouth with her napkin, drained her glass and said, "I've got to go back to the office. Will you be okay?"

As she got herself ready to leave, I reached for the cigarettes, prized one out of the flip-top box, and stumbled to the stove to light it. A few moments later she reappeared and watched as I took a long, defiant, lung-busting drag.

"I'm calling the doctor," she said, framed in the doorway, frowning and shaking her head. "You can't do this."

I nodded my Marlboro Man nod and sat there, elbows propped on the kitchen table, blowing big horns of smoke into the atmosphere.

"I'm calling the doctor," she said, turning to leave. She returned in a few moments and informed me that she wouldn't be home until late. It wasn't until she said "Bye," and I heard the latch click, that I began to wonder what I'd do without her. The consequences of that wonderment prickled and raised a rash of woeful scenarios that made me want to chase after her, shout down the corridor "Come back! Please come back! Don't leave me!"

But I couldn't.

Theresa left me so quickly that I couldn't even protest. It all came down like a breaking wave.

"What's the matter, Caruso? You seem so sad today."

Me? Sad? How could I be sad? I'm a city man!

"Come on. Let's go outside. You need some fresh air, Caruso. You have been inside two days now."

I don't want fresh air. I want walkie-talkies.

"Walkie-talkies?"

I nodded.

"Okay. Let's go. You walkie, I talkie."

I stumbled into the bedroom and fell onto the bed. She followed, sat down and patted my shoulder but that only made it worse. It was unfair. It was so unfair. What did she know about walkie-talkies, anyway? She was a girl! A *mestiza*! *Mestizas* didn't need walkie-talkies. They operated with different sociocultural and gender referents. Boys needed walkie-talkies, especially American boys! They can't be happy or have fun without them; hide from grown-ups, use foul language in secret. Cocksucker! Motherfucker!

"I know what's bothering you, Caruso. It's because you're going away. *Te parales a la palabra melancolía.* I know."

Me? Like the word *melancholy*? I turned my head so I could see her. I was not melancholy! No way was I melancholy!

"It's from Neruda," she explained, still patting my shoulder. "You know who else loves Neruda?"

I shook my head. What did Neruda know about walkie-talkies?

"James Bond. Remember? He sent me a present. A book. *20 Poemas de Amor y una Canción deseperada.* You know it?"

Love poems?

She nodded. "It was sweet, don't you think?"

I shook my head.

"Oh, come on Caruso. Of course it was. He's a berry nice man. In fact, I am meeting him for dinner tonight."

No! Please don't!

"He's a berry interesting man. We have similar interests."

He wants to fuck you!

Her face turned red. She stood up, glowering. "How dare you talk to me like that!" And she marched out of the room and slammed the door.

I wadded up the paper and dropped it onto the floor. First Mr. Langer and now James Bond. Everything was being taken away from me, stolen right out from under my nose by hungry predators with hanging tongues.

Just days earlier, driving upstate with Gina, I had sworn not to let my tongue hang out or become savage in any way. I had sworn to rein in all my base instincts, remain cool in human affairs, even as I was being given a preview of the afterlife.

It wasn't until after we had passed through the gates that I understood we had arrived. They weren't pearly, either; but merely two brick pillars and a sign that said PRIVATE. The road wormed through a patch of woods which, because it was overcast and drizzling lightly seemed as dense, myth-ridden, and primeval as a theology without promises. Gina took my hand and squeezed it lightly. Everything she'd said on the way was now irrelevant and her enthusiasm gave way to a bubbly nervousness which meant we were now on the verge of my future.

The driver glanced in the rearview mirror.

"There's a parking lot behind the main building," Gina told him. "Follow the signs."

I saw no signs. Signs would have been a comfort, proof of ways in and out. Gina squeezed my hand again. I turned to her, wanting to ask if we could go home now. Please? Can we go back?

She must have read my thoughts because she squeezed my hand again and brought it into her lap, which had begun to swell with a promise that I now understood was being reneged on, though Gina's eyes sparkled with the joy of impending motherhood and plans plans plans.

"Here we are," she said. "See? Up ahead?" Suddenly, we were out of the woods and approaching a settlement. There were three buildings set at angles to one another. "Wait'll you see the view. It's amazing. You can see the river, the mountains on the other side." She squeezed my hand hard this time, as though to inaugurate the new reality.

The driver parked the car and Gina told him where he could get coffee and said we'd be no more than an hour. Then we were standing on the steps of the middle building, steps that had been built in grander days for grander occasions by grander men and women and, I was told, commanded a view straight out of the Hudson River School. "Too bad it's cloudy," she said. "I really wanted you to see it."

As if the passive contemplation of landscape were sufficient consolation for the degradation of assisted living! No amount of hermeneutical analysis could interpret away the cold, hard fact that this was a place were people came to be dismissed from life and liberty.

"Hello there," came a cheerful voice from behind us. We turned. Mr. Langer was standing in the French doorway. The smile on his face meant too many things for me to respond. He beckoned us out of the drizzle and shook hands warmly with Gina, then tried awkwardly to demonstrate his willingness to press my flesh as well, if I would only stop clinging to Gina.

But I couldn't.

"Well, how about we start with the tour, then?"

So we toured. Mr. Langer read off the inscriptions all along the way. The place was marked like an airport with signs and plaques all connected by paths and runways for the ambulant dead to taxi down. Gina kept up a steady line of questioning, but I couldn't bring myself to listen, and would probably not have understood, anyway. I knew she was only trying to be pleasant and realistic about things, which was what Dr. Eremita told me I should try to be, too. But how can you be pleasant when your wife wants to have her babies without you? And how can you be realistic on the tour of your own afterlife?

"Think of it as a beginning," Eremita had counciled. A beginning of what? I wanted to know. What use are beginnings when you already know the end? A world of beginnings is incomplete and shapeless, and when you add your ending it suddenly becomes complete and fully formed. You can't pretend shapelessness and incompleteness in a world that has ended, any more than you can pretend you've never seen your wife naked. That was exactly what I had said to Eremita, though she took what I was trying to say all out of context, and figured that I was revealing something deep and hidden by bringing my naked wife into it. But I wasn't. All I was trying to say was that, when you think about it, pretending you're starting over is like pretending you've never seen something you really have seen—like your wife, naked, or knowledge of good and evil, or, simply, THE END. To pretend you're at the beginning, you have to pretend an innocence you forfeited long ago. And the whole time that I was explaining this to her, Eremita was smiling and tapping her pencil and, though she wasn't speaking out loud, I knew she was saying: "Sure. Of course. Right. That's nice, but really, you must see, whatever you say, I know, it's like this . . ."

And that's when I did it. What choice did I have? I was trying to make a point and not getting beyond the glaze of her professional learning. She was the one who had brought up beginnings and endings. All I wanted was for her to understand my point; and all I could do to illustrate was to shatter her innocence. So I pulled down my pants and showed her . . . my *Dichtung*!

Oh my God. Her face. It summed up perfectly all talk of beginnings and endings. It betrayed nothing. Not a thing. She didn't bat an eye or move a muscle, but just sat there and looked straight at me as if to say, "Well now, I suppose you had to do that. But don't think for a minute I am going to react because, you see, I am now confirmed and you, my good patient, now stand fully diagnosed!"

It was beginnings and endings I was making my point about; but as soon as I realized that my argument had been interpreted in terms of a parallel and wholly alien rationality, I became confused, then embarrassed, and I quickly pulled my pants back up.

I think that might have been when my arctic journey really began, not the leave-taking part, but the moment it became an article of my fate. Of course, I wasn't aware of it at the time. The only thing I could hope for was that maybe Eremita would forget; or maybe she'd feel sorry for me and not tell. That was sort of what the look on her face said when we said good-bye.

Theresa was waiting in the outer office to take me home

and all Eremita said was "We're running a little late today. Sorry to keep you waiting," and delivered me over to her with, "It's alright, Michael. Don't worry. Everything is going to be alright."

It was the way she said it, fingering the glasses hanging from her neck and not smiling, but waving to me from someplace just over the horizon, someplace I'd never get to no matter how far I traveled. I'm not Michael Taylor, I wanted to shout. I'm Batman! Because, when you think about it, exposing yourself to your therapist is sort of like being Batman. You pull a mask over your face, draw your cape around, and jump out the nearest window. I punched the button to go back up.

"What's wrong, Caruso?"

I pointed up, punched the button two, three, four, five, six times in that useless pantomime of panic that people go through when they've been trapped in a dumb machine and want to get off. It made me think of Batman again because he never took the elevator, he climbed up the sides of buildings, and even when he wasn't Batman but millionaire Bruce Wayne, he would have pushed the button just once, brushed some lint from his sleeve, and waited calmly for the right moment to make his escape—because having a secret identity allows you to go through life without fear, and that makes you invincible.

So we rode down and people got on, then we rode all the way back up again, in silence, because in crowded elevators everybody becomes flatfooted and they tilt their gazes slightly upwards and away, like spouses evading the issue of unhappy love.

Dr. Eremita was surprised and Theresa confessed that she couldn't explain, either.

"Do you need to use the bathroom?"

I fumbled with pad and pencil. Sorry.

Dr. Eremita seemed to think about it for a minute. Then she said "Apology accepted."

Tears began to well up.

She put her hand on my shoulder. Theresa was shaking her head and looking at her watch because we'd gone way past six. I liked Theresa when we went past six. She went from being all mine, to only partly mine; and the further past six we got the more madly in love I fell. There's a big difference between obediently discharging your duty and cleaving to it because you recognize a higher calling. After six she went from clock puncher to sturdy companion. The more she gave to me the less she kept for herself. Was it greedy of me to see it that way? I think about it now more than I did at the time; but that's only because I did lose her in the end and when you look back over a loss such as that, motives harden like lava and you can read them like geologic events. Sure it's greedy to want. But is it greedy to need? It's greedy to covet, too. But is it greedy to desire?

It was cold and windy outside. Theresa tried to hail a cab but I tugged her arm down. "What now?"

I tugged again and nodded up the block.

"It's late, Caruso. There's no time to walk."

But I insisted. It was autumn. The clocks had been turned back so it was already dark. I breathed long draughts of cool dry air, and yielded to the dunning lights and sounds of the evening rush hour. I strained to walk as uprightly as the people streaming by me, zipped up and buttoned down, nicely turned out with things to do. Theresa sensed something of what I was trying for. She glanced at me out of the corner of her eye and tugged me closer so that, to oncoming traffic, we resembled the rest of the dream unfolding all around. I tried to imagine how Theresa might have responded to my exhibitionism, but I quickly realized that the rhetoric of the act would not have interested her in the slightest. She'd probably have laughed, made a crack about penis size or stinky diapers.

"What you are smiling about, Caruso?"

Her question raised the stakes even higher. Suddenly I was reeling. She held onto me as people steered wide and clear, some with smiles and very pleased to witness an outburst of hilarity, others indifferent to all emotion and meteorological change. Then Theresa began to laugh with me and the atmosphere became positively charged. We staggered up against the side of the building and I loved her more than anything else in the world and began laughing all over again. Then she left me against the side of the building, and stepped to the curb to hail a cab, arm in the air, smiling to herself over all the silly paradoxes and absurd little sputterings she labored under.

Langer's tour began and ended in what he called a "model living arrangement." What it was modeled on I didn't think to ask. As he talked, I kept asking myself if I was mature enough to fit his model; or if it was a question, not of maturity, but dissolution—and what we were being shown was not a structure in which Inner and Outer would find equilibrium, but some trusslike appurtenance to prop up an enfeebled and wholly insignificant self.

Gina opened cupboards and curtains, talked about light and views, the thickness of the walls, the density of schedules, the latitudes of freedom; she talked about furnishings, color schemes, about how often, how many, how much, and Langer answered her every question with a look of deep satisfaction and top-of-the-line conviction. Gina steered me to an easy chair by the window and bade me take in the wonderful view. She sat on the arm, and I was flooded with pictures of her roller-blading and all our days and nights together. I leaned my head against her thigh and closed my eyes so that the pictures would not go away.

"I'll leave you now," Langer said. "Feel free to relax. Get the feel of the place. Take as much time as you like. I'll be in my office."

Then Gina's hand was in my hair. One by one, the pictures dissolved. There was no more roller-blading, no more park, no more aromas of hot wet sidewalk or Chinese restaurant or bus exhaust or hot dog stand. There were no more kissy elevator rides, meet you at the box office get the laundry change the sheets. The entire skyline went black. I felt my diaper swell. Gina's thigh was wet from slobber but she didn't flinch or move. I opened my eyes and saw my mother looking at me through the window, nose pressed against the glass; and though I couldn't hear what she was saying, from her lips I could make out the eight stages of man and something about autonomy versus shame and doubt, and epigenetic charts and wombs mowed with seed, ego integrity versus despair, withering blossoms and annihilation.

Gina stood up, smoothed her skirt and began a second look around. I didn't want to pollute the atmosphere any more than it was polluted and thought about how I might finish the tour with imaginary dialogues and arguments. Or to ask pointed questions like, "Can I have chocolate pudding for dessert? And where are my toys?"

"I'll say one thing, honey," Gina called from the bedroom. "I'm going to insist on a different color scheme. This yellow is just awful." She appeared in the doorway, a look of pleasant possibility on her face. She leaned against the frame, crossed her arms over the swell of her belly. The light hit her face so that I could make out the downy sideburns she told me she once wanted to have removed because the boys at school used to tease her. I wanted to get right down to bare bones with her, let her know how much I loved her and wanted to be loved by her and was willing to endure this pageant of isolation that Knickerbocker Estates was promising only if she would swear not to leave me. For a few minutes I imagined myself there, in that very model living arrangement, all slap happy from the amenities and the view, joking with the staff and pinching the nurses to make an endearing nuisance of myself, with a slate full of organized activities and socials to attend and daily mail from friends and relatives to keep up with. But then Gina flushed the toilet—not the gurgle-burble of ball and tank, but a power-vacuum roar—and I was the guppy sucked down.

Gina took me back to Mr. Langer's office to fill out the forms. I sat there like a disjunctive conjunction, Mr. Either/Or himself, going over the speech I would have given were it given to me to say anything; shifting my weight from buttock to buttock as I sat in my stool, wondering when Langer would stop pretending it didn't stink. Being a lawyer meant that Gina was too busy and comfortable with all the paperwork to notice the smell, either.

Trying to explain walkie-talkies to Theresa wasn't nearly as hard as trying to get her to understand why I needed them. Of course, I wasn't about to mention my actual escape plan, so I just told her I needed them because I wanted them. With the wasties, that's more or less how things are ranked anyway—by want. When you think about it, there is no other way to live. Want and need are only poles in a spectrum that extends way beyond the black. And crying is the shortest distance between them.

"What do you want with walkie-talkies?" Theresa asked.

"You can't walkie too good and you can't talkie at all!"

It was the way she said it that made me roar and wheeze and throw the pillows off the sofa. A fit. That's what it was. But Theresa didn't seem to mind. She just watched me with her arms crossed, tapping her foot. "You finished?"

I went into the bedroom and wrote a note, then crumpled it up into a ball and went back into the other room and threw it at her. I wanted her to know that I could go tit for tat all day long if I had to. Theresa picked the note up off the floor and read it, then she shook her head and laughed. "Because I got a present from Dr. Bond you want one too?"

I nodded my head.

"Caruso! Come. We're going outside for fresh air!"

Okay, I thought. Fine. I'll show you! And I did everything she asked from that point on. Until we were outside where, halfway up the block, I lay down on the sidewalk, and curled up into a tight little ball.

"Caruso! Stop this! Get up!"

People began to gather.

"You need help?"

"An ambulance?"

"Everything alright?"

But I didn't want to get up. Theresa stopped tugging on my arm. "Why you doing this, Caruso? It's no funny. I don't appreciate it. Get up!"

I shook my head, bundled up and trying to breathe just like in physical therapy—*ham sa ham sa ham sa.*

"You sure you don't need help?" A man's voice.

"You want to try?" Theresa asked. "Go on. Try." She had a tone in her voice like the sound of the last judgment. I felt myself beginning to worry, and tried to resist it by keeping up a steady *ham sa ham sa ham sa* and thinking about the walkie-talkies I wanted.

"Come on, buddy," came a man's voice. "Here we go!" Two big hands reached under my arms and suddenly I was leaving the ground.

"It's just up the street." Theresa said. "Over there."

"Jesus, he's heavier than he looks."

All I could see were two big arms thick with hair, and the smell of Aqua Velva aftershave, which awakened something in me like a memory of my father. I felt my legs relax. I began to uncurl in midair. Theresa was holding my cane. "That's it, buddy. That's more like it." And when I turned I saw Walt Whitman—and not all gone to seed like he'd been begging in the subway, but the huge bearded guy who volunteered in hospitals and comforted all those Union soldiers in Fredericksburg and Washington. It was him! Helping me up off the ground like he did the ranks returning, worn and sweaty, dear friend, one by one. He didn't heed me as I let all my weight fall into his hands; and I couldn't even look at him but kept my eyes on Theresa, who was holding my other arm and my cane. Walt Whitman! He uses Aqua Velva! I should have figured as much. It fit more with the body electric than one of those sissy perfumes from Ralph Lauren or even patchouli, which is what Allen Ginsberg used to mask his farts which stank up the whole physical therapy room. Suddenly, I wanted to ask a thousand questions, like what he thought about T. S. Eliot's statement that you cannot value a poet alone but must set him, for contrast and comparison, among the dead. But I realized right away that he'd probably just laugh at me for repeating such a silly idea, because you'd never set the value of a *person* by contrast and comparison with the dead, so why single out poets for such brutal treatment? And then he'd remind me that he wrote, not by contrast or comparison with the dead, but to unite the living and the dead. I felt myself getting mad. I wanted to shout. Fuck T. S. Eliot! And shout it again and again, because there was no comparison in human terms between the two visions, between Whitman, who had lifted me up off the street, and who lived engirthed by the armies of those he loved and who engirthed them in return and charged them full with the charge of the soul—and that spindly little aesthete, who would not have even stepped over or around me out there on the sidewalk, but turned and walked away, because he looked at life through the eyes of his predecessors and lived like a patient etherized upon a table.

Then we were back inside, waiting for the elevator. "You sure? You got him?"

"Thank you. Thank you very much."

When I looked up Whitman was gone. Theresa was standing next to me. I had my cane in my hand. Everything was steady as she goes.

And I still wanted those walkie-talkies.

The Arctic is as much a place as a condition. In traveling there, you don't put obstacles behind you one by one to mark the distance you have come, you pile them up inside, and they become the substance of an interior history that grows and fills you up as you leave the world behind.

I remained in my room, enshrouded in my parka of smoke, beard germinating like frost on my cheeks. My wall was getting further along with each empty package. Thanks to Mister Lee's free delivery service, I was able to procure my Marlboros by the carton, as well as the necessary cigarette lighters, bottles of Ice-X herbal tea, and Delmore's (I rose from the bed, lit a cigarette and walked to the window) glue. You can't stack Marlboro boxes very high without an adhesive; and the reason it took me so long to realize it is that I had been laying them side by side with the idea that I would outline the entire perimeter before building up. It's not that it was such a bad plan; I could have easily smoked my way clear through the 38,000's before running into difficulties. But, as I sat looking out the window one windy night, it occurred to me that it might be better to build upward, wall by wall—joining them only in the final phase of smoking. The practical advantages far outweighed the aesthetic concerns, and although there is something pleasing about the idea of an enclosure that slowly encloses, there is just no practical way of accomplishing it and leaving access to the bathroom. The window was the second important consideration. The closet door, too. My revised plan called for the window to be left to the last phase of construction, along with the doors, which I would have loved to never need or use again, except that without them egress for Gina would have been more difficult than it had already become.

So the countdown continued.

38,881.

It's not such a strange number when you stop to think about it. Not like the numbers 1 or 2. I wish zero could be called a number, but it can't because it's a crucial concept in the idea of Being. I guess you could say 38,881 is a crucial notion in the idea of Being, too; but that would miss the point, because with 38,881 there is no anxiety and with zero—well, you can't contemplate zero without anxiety. There are plenty of ways to *say* zero. You can say nothingness, and when you do you are giving expression to a transcendent expression that can not be qualified, and has nothing to do with null sets, or not-one, or *nihil absolutum,* the absolute nothing which Parmenides called *to medamos on,* or merely the opposite of is. Zero is real cause for anxiety. It's a permanent condition. But trying to fathom it is as pointless as trying to get to the truth of your being by auto-vivisection with mirrors.

All my vital resources were suspended on the ride back from Knickerbocker Estates. I sat in the back of the car like a capsized old man and watched the drizzly world speed by in blur. Gina held my hand and that felt right. She followed the drizzly world out of her own window, and didn't speak a word to me the whole way back to the city. That felt somehow right, too. From time to time the driver glanced back at us in the mirror, and little sparks of mutual recognition flowed between us, a common understanding of the basis of things. It's an acknowledgment that passes often between old people and young children. People in between tend to ignore their proximity to the drooling, pissing, crying, shitting core of mortality. It makes them edgy and impatient and want to hire nurses so they can sit back, hands off, and take pictures, pretend they are acting out of compassion for a unique *individual,* and not simply out of convenience because the crapping, crying wretch has begun to interfere with the Kodak moment.

There were flowers waiting for us when we got back home. A big blooming arrangement sitting there with a card sticking out. They weren't for Gina, but for me! Flowers for me!

"Isn't that sweet," Gina said, and I nodded, wishing she hadn't said it because, although it was a very sweet and considerate gesture, it was also final confirmation of all the papers we had just signed.

The telephone was ringing as we walked in the door. Gina laid the flowers on the sofa and ran to answer it. I sat down to admire them, the miraculous way they have of altering moods, half expecting to hear Gina call from the kitchen, "It's for you, Honey. Günter Grass, calling from Germany. He wants to talk about your book," or, "It's Dr. Eremita, dear. She would love to marry you. Let's cancel Knickerbocker Estates right away." But, instead, she talked for a few minutes, then came into the living room and said, "You'll never guess who that was. Julian Bloom. He's back and wants to stop by and say hello."

Bloom? I tried to remember but could not put a face to the name or a purpose to the visit, so I did what everybody does when an unexpected visitor is announced—I pretended to be busy.

The last thing anybody wants to be seen doing when threatened with a visitor is nothing. Being a real person means being construed by others as an interesting subject because objects that just lie around doing nothing are boring and nobody wants to play with them. I turned on NPR so that I could listen to the rest of the world while I practiced the hokey pokey. My physical therapist, Natalie, said the hokey pokey is good exercise for someone like me. Doing it to the news was my idea. Someone should write an article for Foreign Affairs or the *New England Journal of Medicine* about the hokey pokey—or any dance step, for that matter—because, when you think about it, the best way for an average citizen living in a constitutional democracy to guard and protect himself against the excessive and pernicious bombardment of news and information is to keep in mind that most of it is irrelevant and doesn't matter. Doing the hokey pokey under media bombardment is not just good for the psyche, but for all our democratic institutions. I don't mean Nero fiddling while Rome burns, or those mass exercise classes in China under Mao; but something between the vast similitude interlocking us all, on the one hand, and Li Po, the Tang dynasty poet, who smiled and had no answer to the question: "Why do you live on this green mountain?" because he saw no likeness between his serene heart and the mad human world below.

Bloom appeared in the apartment just as I was putting my right foot in and shaking it all about a report on the political situation in Russia. He brought flowers and kissed Gina on the cheek as he handed them to her, which stopped my hokey pokey in mid-shake. I was about to run over and pull the two of them apart, but I didn't manage quickly enough and, before I knew it, he was coming toward me. "Don't stop. Please. Finish what you're doing."

"Can I get you something to drink, Julian?" Gina asked. "Coffee? A glass of wine?"

I had to sit down on the floor because my right foot was in, and my left foot was still out, and putting them back together was not working too well. Julian offered me a hand and soon we were all sitting down and he was telling us something about having been in Italy, and had just returned the day before, you know how it is, just one thing after another. He didn't look at me as he talked, but at Gina. Then, he broke off and said, "My God, Gina! I just. Excuse me but. Are you pregnant?"

Gina smiled an *embarazadora* smile and put her hand in her lap.

"That's wonderful!" Julian enthused, then turned to me. "Congratulations!" He went on for long enough to reveal an underlying confusion, which he clumsily tried to hide by pulling a pack of cigarettes from his pocket and then putting them back. "Oh, well, I suppose I better not."

"That's okay," Gina said. "I'll open a window."

Julian took the packet out of his pocket, plucked out a cigarette, put it to his lips. When he noticed how closely I was watching, he removed it. "Oh, I'm sorry. I didn't. I forgot. Here. I can wait."

I held out two scissoring fingers.

"You want one?"

I nodded.

"You want a cigarette?"

I nodded my head.

Julian put the cigarette back into the pack. "I didn't mean to start trouble," he said.

"It's not you," Gina said, casting me a look. "We've got a whole smoking problem of our own here."

Julian listened, head propped in one palm, as Gina described the battle she was up against. "Well, it's about time for me to quit, too," he said. "I promised myself I would as soon as I got back. In Italy there was no point in even trying. But now that I'm back."

As he talked, I pulled out my pad and wrote *If death consort with thee, death is to me as life.*

He laughed when I showed it to him, then passed it over to Gina. "Thanks, Mike," he said. "I remember."

"That's good, because I don't," Gina said.

"It's from *Paradise Lost.* Eve offers the apple to Adam, who agrees to doom himself out of love for her. I gave a paper on it a few years ago." He glanced at me with a look of dubious cheer. "I don't know what to say, Mike."

"Well, that's all very nice and enigmatic," Gina said. "But I still don't get it. Unless what you're saying is you want to smoke because you love Julian."

I scissored my fingers and they both laughed like diplomats at jokes in translation, then exchanged uncomfortable glances. Julian slid the cigarette pack into the pocket of his jacket, then looked down at his shoes, then at me, then at Gina. "I can't stop thinking about what has happened to you, Mike. I can't imagine what you're going through." He was squeezing his fingers together as if wringing the words from his hands. As he spoke I felt an absolute clarity of understanding come over me that I couldn't explain and that I wanted to preserve. It was euphoric. That's the only way to describe it; and, even though it disappeared and the words in my head began scattering again, there was compensation in the fact that, somehow, spontaneously, my nervous system had realigned itself, had achieved a momentary coherence. I pulled out my pad to capture some of it in words and wrote as Julian continued. "To think what you must be going through. I don't know. Christ, I don't know what to say."

He looked at me, at Gina, then stood up and began to pace. Gina's eyes were locked on him, her face neutral, as if she were taking a deposition. "I don't know what to say," he repeated several times. "What's there to say? Nothing. I don't know. It's too complicated."

Gina and I exchanged glances—real, meaningful ones, like in the past when communication was so fluid between us that speech felt almost unnecessary; and my heart began to thump in my chest as I saw how preferable it is to profess the superfluity of speech than to find oneself actually speechless. I tried to get this down for Julian Bloom in the context of real and ideal and the absurdity of proposing any identity between them, and how all the lofty talk of pessimism and forgetting and anamnesis can become gibberish and be obliterated absolutely and forever by a simple neurovascular event. As Julian continued pacing and trying to explain why he couldn't explain what he wanted to explain, I scribbled frantically to preserve the euphoria and clarity of the moment. Then, for a split second, I actually thought I felt my bowels. I stopped writing, looked at Gina, who was now observing the proceeding with Sphinx-like amusement, legs tucked up beside her on the sofa. I felt words forming, larynx stirring. I opened my mouth. Everything piled up, crashed together. I heard myself speak.

Gina's head snapped up. "What was that?" She swung her feet from the sofa and ran over to me. "Say it again! Oh, Michael! This is amazing. I don't believe this. Julian! Did you hear? He just spoke! Do it again. Please. Try! Try!"

My head was swinging, swarming, swooning. My mouth was open and Gina was so close, closer than she'd been in I don't know how long—not in proximity of body but enthusiasm of soul. Julian stopped pacing. His hands were jammed into the pockets of his sport coat. He was beaming.

I fixed an obedient look on Gina, as if addressing a teacher or old goddess of the forest—and opened my mouth.

"Theresa?"

No. No. No.

"Ayesha?" Gina asked. "Ayesha? Is that what you're saying? Who is Ayesha? Do I know Ayesha?"

I struggled to repeat.

"Eyes eat?" Julian offered.

I shook my head. No! No! And tried again to repeat. I need to shit! But everything bogged down with the effort. Then, abruptly, my bowels spoke for me, and I flew back into the cloud bank.

"Oh," Gina said, and slid off the arm of the chair. "Oh my. Here. Let me help you."

I took her arm and let her lead me like a duck back to blue Ontario's shore.

Nobody told me when Theresa's last day arrived. We did everything as usual, starting with breakfast and NPR. She asked me if I was feeling better than yesterday. I wasn't sure what she meant since it was already the day *after* yesterday and all you can really do in that situation is take a wait-and-see approach. Anyway, I don't know what to say about time frames, because with the wasties you don't think in terms of frames. You think in terms of phenomenological situations which you arrange into an ontology of appearances that all depend on mood. So even if Gina had told me it was Theresa's last day, it wouldn't have mattered because the information would not have brought order to the incoherence of my day, or humbled me, or made me feel any greater lack of happiness than is accepted and dwelt in already by human beings all over the world who are conscious of their mortality. Theresa understood this and that's why she didn't come bounding in with the announcement that she was leaving. She just went about our regular routine, dropping hints of the fun and games to come.

But did I have to go to physical therapy first?

"Yes," Theresa insisted, and explained for the umpteenth time how it was necessary and meant to make a new man of me. But in spite of all her assurances, things seemed cloaked by hidden purposes, and happened whether or not I chose to believe or doubt.

At therapy, we began with the standard *ham sa ham sa*. Everything seemed just fine between this I and me at first; but lying there on the mat I began to feel self-conscious—not because my knees weren't bending, which they weren't, or because my thumb would not easily touch the tips of each finger, but because Allen Ginsberg had joined our cozy little group and was lying right next to me. There he was, noisily going about his exercises with grunts and groans and moans, distracting the rest of us with his balding, bearlike presence. I rolled onto my side to face him while our yogi master therapist issued her gentle instructions. I wanted to say something to him like, Listen here, Allen. I know all this stuff is old hat to you, and that ever since Aunt Rose powdered your thighs with calamine against the poison ivy while you stood there naked on the toilet seat and were shamed down to the first black curls of your tender manhood, you have stood apart and to the side of this crabbed Western consciousness that inhibits the rest of us, and keeps us from moaning and breathing and reveling in our ductwork with such glorious abandon. So would you please pipe down? But since I couldn't say this to him, staring back at me all vacant and wall-eyed with release—I stuck my tongue out.

He didn't seem to notice. So I did it again, just the little raspberry tip to tease; and when this failed to grab his attention, I rolled out the whole organ for him—AHHHHHHH—like that famous picture of Albert Einstein, and left it dangling as a sign for him, not just to shut up and let the rest of us get on with our rehabilitation, but to inform him that his monopoly on consciousness and his body was not as complete as he believed. I was thinking of Whitman, of course; and I wanted to tell him that I had *seen* the old man unfolded out of the folds like sparks flying from under the wheels of the downtown train, and might even consider inviting him to visit the bard of Camden with me some afternoon, if we could just get a play date together.

AHHHHHHH.

It took some minutes for my rolled-out tongue to have an impact on him, and I was about to give up and face the other way, when suddenly he unrolled his own big red slab and, cross-eyed, he began to waggle it at me. BAHHHHH-HHH. BAAAAAAAHHHH.

So, we lay there on the mat, Allen Ginsberg and me, our

tongues unfurled like bright red banners—AHHHHH-HHH—laughing. A while later we were on the treadmill. Allen and I had bonded, silent old men bewildered by all the machinery in our lives. An intern stood next to each of us, coaxing us on toward a better, healthier cheer.

Hey Allen, I wanted to call over to him. Wanna know how to hump a cow? I struggled forward to nowhere with my wobbly legs, wishing for a way to make us laugh together again. Get yourself a stool, Allen! Remember? And then multiply because and why, divide then by now. Yes! That's the proper way, the e. e. cummings method! He'll tell you. Poet to poet.

"Good. That's very good." The intern's voice. "Great. That's graaaaate! You're doing graaaate."

Allen! Hey! Allen! Do you hear that? We're doing graaate! You and I. Yes. Graaate.

I couldn't take my eyes off of him, a big hairy, barrel-chested rabbi of a man right here in rehab with me. I wondered why our souls hadn't flown off to heaven yet. Or was this heaven? I wanted to ask him, huffing and puffing under the smiling fluorescence of health care professionals. After the session ended, I followed him into the waiting area. I just wanted to be next to him, to soak up some of his superior presence. Allen was steadier on his feet than I was and could talk, though not very clearly or well. I wanted to become his friend.

He was met by a grey-haired lady, who immediately began to fuss and fidget over him. "Stop already," he stammered.

"Yes? Do you need something?" asked the lady, noticing me at last.

Theresa was at my elbow.

"He can't speak," Theresa offered. The woman took stock of the both of us for a moment and then said, "I'm very sorry. I know what you're going through." And then she glanced at Allen. "My husband's speech is only now coming back. Very slowly. It's never too late. No matter what they say. Don't give up hope."

"We will never do that, will we, Caruso?" Theresa smiled and began to tug me away.

"My husband still has trouble making out words," she said, "Come, honey. It's time to go."

But Allen wasn't going to let himself be herded off so easily, even if Aunt Rose had rubbed calamine on his thighs and seen his pubic hair. With an outpatient howl he thrust his tongue out at me AHHHHHHH and I did exactly the same AHHHHHH and suddenly the waiting room was reverberating with hilarious glottal stopping and going, and Theresa was tugging me in one direction and Aunt Rose was hauling her poet nephew in the other. She actually seemed frightened and called for a wheelchair.

When we got home I turned on NPR. They were talking about Iraq. It was sunny outside. I took up my pencil to compose a note. When I found Theresa a while later, she was in the bedroom talking on the phone. She cupped her hand over the receiver. "I'll be finished in a minute. Close the door."

I held my note out to her.

"Let me finish, Caruso. Close the door."

So I went back to the kitchen table and used the time to revise and make my message crystal clear so that she could refer to it in times of doubt, forever and always—sort of the way Dr. Eremita referred to them, except here there would be no room for interpretation. I whittled and whittled and whittled until there was nothing left but the words *I want to be the only one who loves you.*

I could not bear to watch as she read it. I didn't turn to look when she put her hand on my shoulder. I didn't understand a word of what she said to me afterwards, except that it would be our last day together and she was sorry. "So, don't let's be sad, Caruso!" and she put a box on the table. "Here. I brought you a present."

Walkie-talkies!

It was 38,624—cigarette-time, of course. Cigarette-time has numerous advantages over all other modes of time measurement and improves on calendars that advance from season to season, festival to festival, but exclude the maundering philosophical element that is so crucial to living an examined life. Of course, cigarette-time borrows from other calendars, and preserves at its core both sacrificial and eschatological elements. But what makes cigarette-time different is that it preserves the *aeterno modo,* the mode of eternity, by sending it up in a holocaust of smoke.

38,624 marks what I now refer to as the day I went Arctic; and since with calendars you get history as a sort of residual by-product, I am now able to assign dates, mark anniversaries, and anticipate the end of time. 38,624. How come so nice and round? Well, the truth is that it's an approximate date, which is the way it mostly goes with calendars. You always have to adjust, because the owl of Minerva spreads its wings at dusk. With calendars you get dates and with dates you get history.

And history is just another way of saying it's too late.

I was only trying to put some smoke behind me, to accelerate the countdown. I had gone to the closet for a fresh pack, having stacked the latest empty on the wall with a neat little dab of glue. Nearly two-thirds of one wall was completed at this point. I was overcome by excitement and feeling a little nauseated and sore in the throat, and it occurred to me that I could accomplish my goal by other means and still be faithful to the spirit of the process. So I lit two cigarettes, and set one in the ashtray as I smoked the other. The anti-smoking people are exactly right about second-hand smoke; and I realized that it wouldn't be cheating to have an extra cigarette or two burning since, in effect, I was smoking them all anyway! The whole theory of second-hand smoke is greatly misunderstood, by the way. It's not about the rights of the individual, or the quality of the air we breathe or the Surgeon General or the action on the human organism of the toxic alkaloid $C_{10}H_{14}N_2$. What I'm talking about is the smoke itself, the very second-handedness of it, the way it curls up into the atmosphere. It doesn't have to be a cigarette. It may just as well come from a cremation pyre on the banks of the Ganges, or billow from the stacks of a factory or the tail of a rocket, the sheer force of decaying life smoldering across the planet, wafting in the air overhead.

It wasn't long before I'd lit a third and a fourth; then a fifth, a sixth, and so on, until I was back in the closet for another pack, and then another, and pretty soon there were cigarettes burning all around the room—in ashtrays, on plates, lined along the edges of the dresser, bedside tables, the windowsill—all billowing their second-hand smoke into my lungs and the wretched errors of my heart.

I think there were somewhere around ninety cigarettes burning when the front door burst open and the firemen came in. The building superintendent, Vinnie, was right behind, and they were all talking at the top of their lungs. Before I could hide under the covers someone was screaming "Jesus fucking Christ will you look at Dis!"—and I knew he didn't mean the god of the Gauls, or Hell, but at the effect on the atmosphere of ninety or so cigarettes. They all piled into my little room, stubbing out smoldering butts by grinding them into the floor with their big boots and saying the things that firemen say when their anxieties are suddenly and unexpectedly relieved.

"What the fuck! Open the windows. Check the mattress. Look under the bed," until every cigarette had been stubbed out and the apartment searched. They talked on walkie-talkies and the Chief came up and began asking questions but Vinnie pulled him aside and told him "Forget it. He can't talk. I'll take care of everything," and the Chief said something about social services but Vinnie said, "He lives here with his wife. It's alright. I think she's a lawyer or something."

I was sitting in bed like Proust or some mad potentate with the covers all bunched up around me. Cold air was blowing through the open windows. Vinnie turned a grave look on me and shook his head. "You gotta cut out the smoking, my friend." He ran his hands over the surface of the wall, then turned his attention to my wall in progress. "I heard of guys collecting cans and bottles and whatnot." He fingered the boxes, marveling at how many and how high they were stacked. "We had a guy once. Never mind. You don't even wanna know." He made another inspection of the place before coming back into the room. "I don't know, Professor. It don't look too good, you know what I mean? Someone oughta be looking in on you." He shook his finger at me and said, "I'll be back in a few minutes. No more stupid tricks, Professor. I'm warning you." And then he left, slamming the front door behind him.

I had wandered into the tundra, that remote interior place where a broad ice-sheet extends to a horizon ridged with glaciers, where glittering bergs of blinding white reach thousands of feet into the sky, everything in movement, reverberating in a stillness that only amnesia can breach. I knew that Mr. Langer would be coming for me. I knew it even before Gina told me. With the wasties, all landscapes converge in this interior arctic whiteness, and half of getting there is not knowing how you made it, and half of being there is not knowing the way back. People have always wondered about the mysterious mechanism, the internal compasses and clocks that migratory animals possess which allow them to traverse vast distances along exact routes over and over and over again. When you have the wasties, living takes on this migratory aspect, and you come to rely on the same atavistic impulse, because memory is the core that both sustains and governs the use of it. I'm not talking about specific memories here—hunting, feeding, mating memories; because those are exactly what is lacking when you make your home in the vast arctic wastes of the wasties. Even high up in my room during hours on end of sitting at the window where the pigeons cooped and my toes pushed their way through my socks, I knew Mr. Langer was coming for me. Gina promised heaven in an end to all the waiting; but I saw through what she meant, and know she was just trying her best not to be too mean.

There are no winding streets in Manhattan. When the urge to run away overcomes you, there aren't many alterna-

tives except to follow a circuitous route dictated by something arbitrary, like a newspaper blowing on the breeze, or
an injured pigeon, or someone who looks like someone you
think you used to know. There was nothing left for me to do
but play the injured truant and go in search of new hopes
and dreams.

I made my way to Mister Lee's to thank him for all the
free delivery and pass the time of day.

"No. You. No more. No more." He came out from behind
the counter. I tried to resist but only managed to irritate
him. "You no more customer. No more cigarette. Nothing."
People pushed by me to finger the produce stacked on
either side of the door. Mister Lee wagged his finger. "You
no welcome my store. Go away."

He maneuvered me a short way up the sidewalk, and I
could feel him watching me as I followed the noisy rill of
the street eastward. I had trained my eyes to scan both
banks of the street, to filter out distracting features of flora
and fauna along the burnished pavement. A three-legged
mote of dust in a gale, I made it across icy Columbus
Avenue and Broadway. I passed Sleepy's and Grey's Papaya,
Malachy's Bar, Ruxton Towers and Oliver Cromwell. The
sun streamed through the clouds and my coat beat against
my sides like wings or flaps. People swirled past in a convection of currents and purposes. Every time I paused to catch
my breath, I saw brief flashes of meaning in the movement
all around. I shuddered, and launched myself on the eastward currents into Central Park.

You don't go to the Arctic. You have it visited upon you.
Even with the essentials all in order—proper clothing, ciga-

rettes, food and cooking supplies—you don't experience it as an animal, but as a vegetable, which is more or less what you become after wandering for too long in the permafrost without money or a picture ID. If you're lucky, they take you straight to a shelter. But that didn't happen to me. The night was freezing. The Reservoir looked like a solid sheet of ice. I had become separated from Muir and my cigarettes, in just about that order, somewhere near the Great Hill. We had wandered north together to listen to what Muir called music, but which sounded to me like wind in the trees. It was pitch dark when we were separated, and even though I had the matches, it was immediately clear that he'd abandoned me.

We'd had a good time together. He saw me smoking on a bench and asked if he could have one, too. He looked thinner than the first time we met, on the day he helped Theresa fetch my cane from where I'd dropped it in the glacial moraine. I was surprised to see him. As he sat down and lit his cigarette, I wanted to ask if he was just returning from his thousand-mile walk to the Gulf of Mexico. But Muir (which means wasteland in Scottish, and made me think we had something in common) was not very talkative. He seemed content to sit quietly and smoke my cigarettes. My coat pockets were crammed full. I was a committed, full-time smoker. I had my walkie-talkies with me, too. They're pretty much useless, by the way—but only in the sense that I can't use them. I discovered this on the very first day I had them, which was also my last day with Theresa.

We met James Bond on the steps of the museum on that miserable last day. He wanted to take us to see the new planetarium; but I was too frightened by the implications of a handicapped-accessible model cosmos and, in any case, wanted to play with my new toys. So we went to the park.

Theresa was spilling over with affection, every bit the requited lover. She walked between us, holding on to Bond's arm while I stumped along with my cane, trying my best to keep apace and rise to the occasion. People are always beautiful when in love. The universe is in order, everything in it's place. There was nothing left for me to do but banish my jealousy and resentment. I'll even admit that the pain of it all gave me some pleasure. Yes it did. The weather was good. Bond was talking to Theresa in Spanish. I hardly understood a word that passed between them; but the subtext oozed with fresh, ripe desire. They were completely unaware of anything outside themselves. I recognized the state from my roller-blading days with Gina. The world rolled by underneath while we stood motionless atop it, holding hands! The language we spoke was a polyglot of hidden meanings and revealed urges that drew us close, each to the other, never stopping, never over. Whole worlds come into being during these moments of fresh, exuberant love; worlds that always vanish, become lost. Even with memory to serve you, there is no joy in recalling them; only insoluble melancholy.

I began to feel euphoric again. Contractions began in my mouth and throat that felt like words waiting to be expelled. I made for the nearest bench and sat down.

"Are you tired, Caruso?"

I couldn't get the no out, and didn't want to say yes, either. Theresa broke away from Bond and sat down next to me. "Are you alright? You look uncomfortable."

Bond sat down, concerned, and also curious. I began to shake. My mouth fell open but no words came. I heard a laugh break loose and I flapped my hand, begging them to be patient.

Theresa put a hand on my knee. "Easy, easy. Relax now. Take a deep breath."

Bond was excited. The glances of passersby sent a thrill through me like the thrill of performance. I closed my eyes to see if the words might appear on my eyelids where I could read and pronounce them aloud.

"Shplay?" Bond guessed.

"Splay?" Theresa asked. "Splay what?"

I nodded. Yes! Yes! And the rest tumbled out.

"Jambon? You mean ham?"

I shook my head. No! Not ham!

"James Bond!" Bond said, standing up.

Yes! I was nodding, nodding, shaking, nodding.

"He said 'James Bond!' "

I nearly fell over from nodding, tried to stand up; but Theresa took my hand and guided me back down.

"Let's play James Bond? He wants to play James Bond!"

I pointed to Theresa's bag. She smiled a smile that obliterated all smiles and took out the walkie-talkies. "He wants to play 007. With these," she explained, and gave one to Bond. He examined my brand-new toys. "Motorolas," he said. "They're good."

I fumbled with buttons. A loud hiss erupted, then a stream of static. Bond sat down next to me. As Theresa looked on, he examined the buttons and explained their function. He set the channels, demonstrated the FM radio, the altimeter, the barometer, the clock, and the compass. I can't describe the pleasure of hearing static over a brand-new set of walkie-talkies except to say that it's like getting a sudden glimpse of the highest degree of cleverness and being invited to share in the secret. It's not a father/son moment, as much as the moment when the father becomes a son again, and initiates an infinite regress of fathers and sons back beyond beginnings where all play originates. Yahooo!

I struggled to get up, brushing Theresa's hand away. Come on! You go that way, I'll go this way! Go hide. No! I'll go hide!

Bond's face was alight with polite and confused enthusiasm. His eyes twinkled and he scratched his greying goatee. "I'm not sure," he said. "What exactly do you want to do?"

Theresa seemed confused as well and took my arm, tried to maneuver me back onto the bench. He had to ask? I couldn't believe he had to ask! I marveled at the beautiful device in my hand, turned it over, caressed its buttons, purred. Motorolas. Bond and Theresa were waiting for an answer. But there is no way to explain play. You either get it and tear off in the general direction, or you don't, and end up standing around hating your toys and unsure of your friends. What was there to explain? Did I have to lead him by the hand and tell him who to be? He was James Bond, I would be Goldfinger. Or he could be Doctor No, and I would be 007.

I was still trying to sort out who would be whom and getting nowhere when Bond said, "I have an idea. You and Theresa go down to the Great Lawn and I'll go look for that pileated woodpecker. There have been two or three other sightings but I haven't seen it for myself since that first day. We'll keep each other posted by walkie-talkie."

"A good plan," Theresa agreed, offering me her hand. I noticed that she was wearing new earrings. At least, they looked new, and sparkled and set off her happiness in a way that made her look like Frida Kahlo. When happiness is set off by jewelry like that, flaunting is allowed. You don't ask questions and you try not to stare. You want to participate in both the gifts and the happiness; but you play by the rules and pay the compliment, which is the price of wanting it all for yourself. You say: How pretty, how nice, you look radiant and stunning, instead of Gimme that! I want that! Mine! Mine! Mine!

"Shall we go?" Theresa asked.

Bond stood up and put his walkie-talkie to his lips. "Let's go," whistled from the one I was holding. It startled me, and everyone laughed.

Sure, I wanted to have fun. Theresa and I walked to the Great Lawn. On the way Bond's voice came over my handset. "Starling, morning doves, nest of crows." But I wasn't paying much attention because *Mr. Spaceman* began coursing through my head. Hey, Mr. Spaceman / Won't you please take me along / I won't do anything wrong. Bond's voice kept interrupting with the names of birds, but I was thinking of The Byrds. Gina liked The Byrds, too; but hadn't really listened to them much until she met me. She had been a punk during the Carter administration. Then came law school and she started listening to chamber music, and met me when The Byrds were largely forgotten, except for certain members of the faculty who liked to date themselves by reference to popular culture and to hint broadly about the good old days of drugs and sexual promiscuity. By then, condoms had become de rigeur throughout the culture. Gina and I only stopped using them after we'd agreed to be tested for HIV and get married.

Theresa and I lay down on the grass. The sun was high. It was Indian summer. We lay there on the ground, in love with the light and the air, like varietals of wheat that can flourish in ennui.

I brought that exact picture with me to the Arctic to help stave off the cold. But it didn't work. I followed Muir. He didn't talk, and liked that I couldn't. Having cigarettes and nothing better to do was all the excuse I needed. But I knew I'd have to prove myself a perfect wonder of a dog along the way. I knew I'd have to measure up; endure the cold like a bear and swim like a seal and not run off after ducks and small animals but just supply the cigarettes and not beg for food or anything else in return.

There were so many questions I wanted to ask, landscapes I would have loved him to describe. What did it feel like to see huge trees bending over in a mountain gale? How do the junipers and dwarf pines survive on the peak of Mount Shasta, while the silver pines that grow in the lower elevations get blown down with the slightest wind? Had I asked, I'm sure he would have told me about all the giant storms he witnessed, right down to the fragrances in the air. But, of course, I couldn't ask. Our silences were broken only by "Gimme another cigarette, man." And I would fumble and fish in my coat pockets as he sat with bony legs crossed, doubled over his lap. His beard grew in wild wisps and his hair was like a brush fire. He sucked his cheeks in as he smoked, and the deep bone structure of his face was revealed. I enjoyed imagining him beside some clear mountain stream quietly observing the lichens and the moss beneath the flowing water.

"What's your name, man?" He asked me at some point.

I didn't have a pencil, so there was nothing for me to do but offer him another cigarette. He resumed his doubled-over posture, smoking and contemplating the tops of his worn-out sneakers. After a while he asked, "You got any money?"

I took out all my cigarettes and held them up for him to see.

"That's cool," he grumbled. "Me neither." And suddenly I remembered his description of the villages of the dead on Saint Lawrence Island and the ghastly scene of shrunken bodies clothed in rotting furs lying side by side in the huts they had starved in; and how Nelson the bone man went collecting skulls to send to the Smithsonian like a boy out gathering pumpkins. I tried to imagine what I might have felt, seeing human defloration up so close—in the words of the Eskimos, "All mucky. All gone. All mucky." The coincidence of Inner and Outer applies to landscapes as much as to human beings; and watching Muir smoke on the bench I could actually see into him—not his bones, but the surrounding landscape, the city we were gathered in, and that was gathered in us, all its richness and its sorrow rushing in our veins like blood that could be drawn. Only the experienced observer can see how inside and outside cohere like this. With the wasties you get the view everywhere you look.

"You know anything about rockets?" Muir asked after a while.

I shook my head.

"That's too bad." He sucked the last bit of smoke out of his cigarette and ground the butt out with his foot. I pulled my cigarettes out and he took another one. I waited for him to continue talking but he just smoked the next cigarette down to the filter, ground it out. "You smell like shit, man," he said after a time. "Wanna hear some music?"

I nodded.

"Come on," he said.

I followed as closely as I was able. My right side wasn't co-operating with the rest of me and I fell further and further behind until, finally, I lured him back by waving a pack of cigarettes in the air. I offered it to him and he accepted with the usual "Thanks, man." Then he grabbed me. I felt his hands rifle through the pockets of my coat. I tried to resist but only succeeded in falling down. "Sorry, man," he said, and knelt down beside me. He took all my cigarettes and my wallet. He deliberated for a moment about the walkie-talkies, then decided against taking them and helped me to my feet. "Hate to do this to you, but it's cold as shit out here, man."

Yes, it was cold. I tried to recapture some of the warmth of the Indian summer afternoon with Theresa—and not by Muir's metaphor of shit, which frightened me and revealed the truth of my predicament—but by remembering Theresa and how we lay there in the sunshine. She was more talkative than usual on that last afternoon together. It was as if she wanted to show me a glimpse of her new life without telling me what her actual plans were. I didn't say so, but I already knew that she would probably end up as another skinned bird in his collection, any of several North American titmice having the top of the head black—a chickadee, most likely, an exotic one, unknown to science, but all too well known to poetry, especially love poetry, especially Neruda's, with which she had been trapped and caught like dew in a cupped flower.

Bond's voice squawked on the handset. "Hey, folks! I'm standing just at the edge of the pond. You'll never guess who I've just run into. Over."

Theresa brightened and she reached for the little radio. "The bird. He found the bird."

141

"Do you read me? Come in. Over."

Theresa held the handset to her lips and said, "*Sí. Bueno?*"

There was a silence. She smiled at me, holding the thing right up against her lips as if trying to send kisses over it. Then I saw that she was still holding the transmit button. I pointed but she merely smiled a preoccupied smile, waiting, waiting, waiting. You have to let go of the button! I tried to scoot closer but my scoot came on more like a lunge and I knocked her down and fell on top of her, which came as such a surprise to both of us that it took several seconds of grunting and flailing before I was able to touch my lips to hers. She heaved me aside and scrambled to her feet, brushed the grass from her with curt swipes and unable to put her irritation into articulate speech beyond "Aye yi yi."

The walkie-talkie had landed a few feet away. Bond was squawking, "The nest. I think I found the nest! This is very important. I'll meet up with you a little later. Over."

Theresa stood over me, ignoring the radio. "Why, Caruso? Why you did that?"

I lay there like a pile of fresh shad roe. I didn't know why and wanted to say so. But I couldn't. And Bond kept repeating himself over the radio—"Do you read me? Do you read me? Do you read me? Over"—words as meaningless to me that afternoon, as the walkie-talkies were useless to me later, in the trek northward.

Muir was essentially a Luddite and preferred the company of trees and mountains and glaciers to men. I tried to follow him, not because I wanted my things back, but because I still had hopes of reaching the Pole with him. I fell further and further behind until, just before darkness came on, he disappeared from sight. I pressed on, hoping to see a kindled fire or even the flare of a match in the distance. But he was gone.

The cold grew more intense and breathing became difficult. When the arctic night comes on, it comes on for the rest of the year. You can't see anything but the blanketed vastness and you are nothing but a fine particle drifting freely. The constellations turn around Polaris, yet even that ancient anchor and the Big Dipper and Ursa Major and all the familiar stars in the sky offer no solace. I sat down on a bench and trembled, afraid of Gog and Magog, lost in the country of the Great Bear. I was hungry and thirsty and wanted a Coke. I would have given anything for one. My left side seemed more detached than usual, and I might have drifted to sleep but realized I needed to keep moving to stay warm. So I got up and started back south, thinking of the Great Lawn and the concerts I had gone to there with Gina. She was surprised and tickled to learn that, yes, the author of that post-everything opus maximus liked sappy old James Taylor and knew the words to "You've Got a Friend" by heart!

I stumped onward, neither fully awake, nor yet asleep, but somehow enlivened by the creeping awareness of a dream I wanted to enjoy. I saw the sparkling lights of Central Park South and felt warmed by the sight. My open overcoat beat dithyrambs against my thighs. Several times that day I had wanted to ask for help in buttoning it, but even had I been able to ask him in plain English, Muir would probably only have jeered at me for needing a coat in the first place. He told me all he needed in the wilderness was a canvas sack, a few dry crusts, and a parka, which doubled as his bed. With the wasties, you understand that point of view. You know what it is to go in silence, without baggage, avoiding hotels and chatter. With the wasties, you discover that travel is neither a means to an end nor an end in itself, but a permanent state of relations between you and the world. Muir and I had sat and smoked together, not as companions, or men, or children of God, but as consequences of this traveling state of relations. He had gone his separate way in keeping with this, and I was going to Knickerbocker Estates in keeping with this, and Theresa was being seduced by James Bond in keeping with this, and nobody ever lives happily ever after but simply keeps on keeping with this first principle of transient existence—which knowing about gets you exactly nowhere.

When I arrived at the Great Lawn my heart began to beat faster. I walked to a point near the epicenter and sat down. The softball diamonds, the turrets of Belvedere Castle rising up on the banks of the marsh, Cleopatra's Needle and the constellations of Midtown were my only points of reference, except for a slowly erupting pastiche of memories that included concerts, that last afternoon with Theresa, my Motorolas, Vinnie the super, Mister Lee and my Marlboro clock.

It's too easy to say I was rescued. But that's what everyone likes to say. Gina was the first to put it that way and that's okay with me because it allows her to affirm a particular version of ordinary life along with all its corollaries. The doctors and staff at Knickerbocker Estates took up the theme of rescue right away; but only because their daily regimen presupposes a paradigm toward which it is their job to strive with every bit of catastrophic health coverage and long-term religion they can lay their hands on. But I wasn't rescued. I can't say what the exact combination of words or insights is, or what must be done to trigger them. It may just be that having spent the day in a fouled diaper, I became attuned to the higher purity of my being. There are plenty of precedents for such transformations. But with the wasties you don't have to spend forty days in the desert eating insects. A cold night in Central Park breathing in the sumptuous perfume of your own shit will do.

At first, I was only aware of being patted down by hands. Many hands, all over. Had Muir returned? Did he want more cigarettes?

"Hello! Can you hear me?"

"Check his pulse."

"Is he breathing?"

"Hello! Can you hear me?"

Words flooded my head. Peace is always beautiful. Everything in the dim light is beautiful. I felt a fluffy beard brushing against my cheek as someone leaned over and brought my arms up to my chest. A thumb pried open a lid and a bright light stabbed my eyes. It was Whitman, his face lit by spots of kindled fire, a procession winding around me.

"Get him a blanket," he said. Then the light was gone and I was passed in all directions. The lover, the son, the sleeper, red lights blinking atop the buildings, the gentle undulation of wheels over turf, then smooth pavement, lamplight filtered through the bare limbs of trees and Motorolas squawking. "We're bringing him in. No I.D."

Even with walkie-talkies it was hard for James Bond to find us out there in the sporting vastness of the Great Lawn on that last afternoon. "Do you read me? What's your position? Over." He kept asking, but Theresa didn't know walkie-talkie talk and I couldn't explain it. It wasn't that she wasn't modern, just that she lived in a twilight of tradition, and walkie-talkies were as incomprehensible and unnecessary to her as psychoanalysis and roller blades. She got frustrated and stood up, waved her arms until, at last, Bond's voice crackled, "There you are. I see you."

Bond had a whole picnic with him. As he pulled all the goodies out of the bags, Theresa leaned over and kissed him on the lips. It wasn't because of the food and the goodies, but because she was in love with him, and would have kept kissing him under the endless sky of the Great Lawn if it weren't for me there watching them.

"What you giggling at, Caruso?" she asked, handing me a sandwich. She wasn't expecting an answer. Even if she was, I couldn't have given it; and I can't explain how giggling and jealousy go together either; except, maybe, as a way of weaving things together, while trying to break them apart at the same time.

The picnic was fun. Theresa and Bond were nice to me, even though I could tell they were just waiting until I was gone before they became themselves with each other. We didn't have a blanket or a Frisbee or a kite, but I didn't mind. You don't always have to loft something into the air to have fun playing outside. I had my Motorolas. Bond talked with Theresa in Spanish. I just ate my sandwich and listened.

Which is pretty much how it was after I woke up on a gurney in a hallway in Bellevue, hearing Spanish mixed with English, and Motorolas, and doctors being paged. There was a complicated cigarette taste in my mouth and I tried to sit up but couldn't. Then I noticed I had a needle in my arm and a few minutes later a man stopped by and began to ask me questions. It was Ralph Ellison. My pulse jumped. I wanted to remind him that we'd met years ago at a reception. "It's me, Mr. Ellison. Remember me? Remember?"

He didn't show any sign of recognition and took my pulse, fixing a kindly look on me. "How do you feel?"

Mr. Ellison! I wanted to shout. It's me! Remember? The reception? NYU? We talked. You and me.

"Can you hear me?"

I nodded, eagerly.

"Do you have any pain?"

Pain. He wanted to know if I had pain! I would have liked to laugh but managed nothing more than a grin that must have looked a little fishy to him because the next thing he did was shine a light into my eyes.

"Can you tell me your name?"

That put me completely over the edge. I began to laugh. My name! The author of *The Invisible Man* was asking for my name! Don't you know me? I struggled to speak but the more I struggled the graver his look became and the more distant he seemed. I wanted to remind him of his own words about seeing with the inner eye and being unseen and merely a phantom of other people's minds. I wanted to tell him how I, too, understood the paradox involved in rejecting the logic of idealism, as well as the empiricist infrastructures of Marxism and the analytic schools, and finding yourself right back where you started. I wanted to tell him that he himself had said all sickness was not unto death and neither was being invisible—which is to say, yes, seeing is believing, but being unseen brings another way of believing into existence which includes elements of divinity and a transcendent madness. I wanted to tell him that with the wasties you become a particle-less entity, too. Just like the Invisible Man. Oh, Mr. Ellison! Don't you recognize me? I might be white but oh my soul is black. Don't you know me? We met at a reception. Don't you know who I am? Don't you remember?

In the end, parting with Theresa was traumatic. No! Don't take her away! She's mine! She's mine! Of course, I couldn't speak the words but they were in my heart. We had come home from the picnic in the park. Theresa wanted to introduce Bond to Gina. I don't know why, but it probably had something to do with some form of pride over the new facts of her life and the grand opera she envisioned for herself. He was extra courtly in every way and permitted himself to peruse the bookshelves while Gina and Theresa fetched glasses and wine from the kitchen.

"You have quite an interesting library here," Bond said, took down a book and opened it.

I had taken the batteries out of my walkie-talkies and was not having much success getting them back in. As my struggles with them became more and more spastic, Bond put the book back on the shelf. "Here. Let me help you," he offered.

But I stuffed the handsets and batteries between the sofa cushions. Go away. I can do it all by myself! We stared each other down for a moment or two, then Bond stuck his thumbs into his ears, flapped his palms, and blew a raspberry. His face was so scary! A frightening expression of exacerbated nerves.

"What's the matter?" Theresa asked.

I opened my mouth to speak but only squeaked and began to drool.

"It's my fault," Bond said a little sheepishly, but clearly fascinated. "I made a face."

"It's alright, Caruso." Theresa sat down beside me and gently rubbed my upper arm. Gina appeared carrying a tray with a wine bottle, three glasses and my sippy cup. "Is everything alright?"

"Just a little misunderstanding," Bond offered.

"Well, here. Maybe this will help settle everybody down." Gina handed me a Virgin Mary, which was my favorite thing to drink out of a sippy cup because of the way the viscous and slightly lumpy tomato juice rumbled through the valve. She set the tray down and poured the wine. They hoisted their stemmed glasses in a *salut* to all their efforts on each other's and my behalf. I watched from my corner of the sofa, drinking from my sippy cup, the wordless victim of their civilities. To thee in thy future! Thy beautiful world of assisted living, endeared alike, forever equal. Here here!

Bond then took the floor and talked for a while about the marvelous time we had had chasing woodpeckers in the park. The more he talked, the less and less professorial he became until, finally, his appearance became completely goatlike. Everything about him was pointed, his greying goatee, the horns on his head, dangling little pee pee between his legs, and his mannerisms of speech that banished all fantasy from life and turned everything into a question-and-answer session. Then I saw him on top of Theresa with his back all bunched up, grunting away like a satyr and it wasn't just that, but also the fact that he was taking her away from me that made me forget about the Motorolas and all the James Bond we'd played in the park and the picnic, and just as he turned his back to address some further remark to Gina, I hurled my sippy cup and—bull's-eye!—hit him right on the back of the head.

Labeling things is a way of achieving a sort of ersatz oneness. By labels I don't mean mere names; and by things I don't mean trees, buildings, ideologies—I mean the veridical images of the stuff that makes you human! It can be anything, come from just about anywhere. A good labeler understands this, begins with particular, and struggles toward universal, because body parts are as important as the mind that operates them, and great fun to play with, too. I'm not just talking cocks and cunts, but heads and laps and every cubic hour of light spent looking at yourself in the mirror, wondering about all the other selves that came across each other to get you here because, with the wasties, you understand that the sum of your body parts is far less than the more you have become.

Sometimes I see squirrels that look like weasels playing out on the lawn at Knickerbocker Estates. You don't have to have to be a prisoner of assisted living to know that a member of the genus *Mustela,* of the family Mustelidae resembles a cunning, sneaky person, which piece of intelligence I came slowly to appreciate when Gina brought Julian Bloom along on her very first visit to see me. They breezed in together as if, all their lives, they had been waiting for this opportunity to seize me by surprise and shower me with hugs and cheer and gifts to make a better man of me. It was Gina who did most of the breezing, actually. Julian remained awkwardly in the background as I stared at him from the back of Gina's embrace. I can't say what time it was, or day or month or year; but by the tautness of Gina's belly I could tell that it had been more than weeks and less than months since the day she had dropped me off at Knickerbocker Estates.

"How are you feeling?"

I wasn't sure what she expected of me. I tried my best to force a smile. This thrilled Gina. She kissed me, which had the effect of summoning Julian from the sidelines. "Hi, Mike," he said. Then he laid a package in my lap.

I looked up at him. For me? A present? My heart began to rollick with all the sweet delight of the good ship Lollipop.

"Go ahead," Gina said, arms crossed over her tumescence. "Open it."

Not another book, I wanted to shout, glancing at the highly praised and heavily annotated translations lined up like bricks on the shelf. I fumbled with the wrapper, achieved little more than a tear here and a rip there. "Let me help you," Gina offered, and sat on the arm of the Laz-E-Boy. As she carefully slid a manicured finger underneath the taped edges, our eyes met, and it felt like her fingers were gliding along the edges of my heart. Julian took up a sentry post just behind her and looked on happily as the wrapping was gently peeled away and the gift exposed. I looked at it down there in my lap, then up at Gina. "Your book," she said. "It's out in paperback."

"Hot off the press," Julian offered. He smiled benevolently, rocked back on his heels as if all that ever came down to anything always came down to this. "They did a great job on the cover."

"Isn't it wonderful?" Gina asked and picked it up. She put it in my hands and held it there, eyes moistening, nostrils pumping, growing red. I watched the tears flow down her cheeks and felt my own face grow hot and cold. Oh Gina, what could I whisper to you? What could I say? What more could you know of me or I of you that would take us out of this predicament for long enough to matter? I wanted to see daybreak in her eyes. Not tears. I wanted her to feel the reverberations of my heart. Not rippling waves of pity. I wanted all the nectars and juices of love to flow again between us. Not this monosaccharine glutamate of tears.

I slid the book from my lap and, with Julian's help, managed to stand up and move to my little easy-access desk in front of the window. It's my favorite place to sit, where I make up labels and watch the weasels out on the lawn. I could feel their eyes on my back, see Gina wiping her tears away with the back of her hand, smell Julian's body lotions and the odors of requited lust it failed to mask.

152

Where are the toys?

"Toys?" Gina asked. "What toys?"

Bath toys.

"Bath toys? You never said anything about bath toys."

I want toys.

Julian hurried over, helped me back onto the chair I had nearly toppled off in trying to write. "No problem, Mike. You want bath toys, we'll get you bath toys," he said.

I could feel Gina's hands on my shoulders and sense the bewildered winks passing between Julian and her. "What sort of bath toys would you like?"

A tugboat and a duck that squirts.

"Fine, honey. I'll get them to you right away. As soon as I get home."

"Do you have help in the bath?" Julian wanted to know in a friendly sort of way.

I would have liked to satisfy his condescension by describing how I am, in fact, helped in and out of it every day; how my back and neck get scrubbed and how they'd probably wash my nuts too, if I asked them, which I bet Gina would never do for you, never never never no matter how many times you may have motherfucked her by now.

Then Paulette came in with juice and cookies. It's one of the features of Knickerbocker Estates that distinguishes it from assisted living around the world. You get snacks. With enough notice, whole meals can be delivered to you and your guests, so that visits subsume the aura of bona fide social engagements and fool people into wanting to come back again and again and again. Fooling people isn't something you do with the wasties. Not intentionally. It just happens as a sort of by-product of behavior. There aren't any calculations involved, because with the wasties cruelty isn't an abstract category of conduct. Everything is done forth-rightly and with the best of intentions, yet has a tendency to unravel with the same sort of wild momentum that makes love interesting—not erotic, exactly, but something very similar involving Inner and Outer, seen and unseen, giving and receiving, recklessness and caution.

I wasn't trying to become invisible as I lay on the gurney in the corridor at Bellevue; yet somehow that is what I became. It wasn't just Ralph Ellison who failed to recognize me before disappearing into the ether of the hospital, but the entire staff of the city, all of society, in fact. It was mainly because I lacked money and identification; and although being poor and having no bureaucratic proof of existence are two very different things, in combination the result is complete transparency. When you become transparent there's not much you can do. You can run around waving your arms in the air, you can yell, hoping to get seen; or you can do what most people without money or proof of existence do: Hold out a cup, clutch your heart, and sing.

It just happened. Don't ask me how or why because I can't say. I have certain suspicions, but they don't get much beyond what I just said about fooling and becoming stuck at the mercy of a heartless bureaucratic/medical ontology requiring paperwork, and at the same time occupying a gurney in a crowded corridor at Bellevue; not just occupying, but actually strapped in and hooked up to an IV, the drip on which was of more concern to the occasional nurse or intern passerby than was I, the receptacle at the other end of the plastic bag.

"Can you tell me your name?" I was asked again and

again; and, every time, I shook my head and was treated to reprise after reprise of woebegone, post-traumatic, kid-glove care-giving. I was just beginning to adjust to invisibility, to actually savor the sensation, which is hard to describe except, perhaps, by contrast to ways of believing. My case was fairly complex. A man without identification is simple enough, but a man lacking the necessary means to provide an account of himself is a category of existence that challenges conventional ideas of what it is to *be*. And that, I suppose, is the essence of both the wasties and invisibility—a state wherein the conditions for being are only partially fulfilled.

That's when I began to sing.

It all just happened somehow. My IV had just been checked by Marianne Moore, although I didn't recognize her at first because she wasn't wearing her Chevalier de l'Ordre des Arts et des Lettres, but just a simple name tag. I wanted to sit up, but couldn't. She checked my pulse, asked how I felt. In her eyes I could see her saying "Tell me, Tell me." I should have loved to explain that I couldn't tell her, but since it's impossible both logically as well as physically to say what you can't know, I closed my eyes. And when I opened them I was singing. *Taareeeessssaaaa! Taareeeessssaaaa!* And kept singing it as loudly as I could and with all the feeling I was capable.

Nurse Moore was at my side almost immediately. A flood of emotion seized up in me that said I'd had enough. But I couldn't stop. I was too astounded, and wanted to finish the refrain, which, after struggling and struggling, at last came out on key and in perfect pitch, to the utter amazement of Nurse Moore. *I just met a girl named Taareeeessssaaaa!*

This set in motion a whole series of actions and events.

Mostly, I had no clue what was happening. Somehow, Nurse Moore and a doctor figured out my problem based on drooping facial muscles and other clues in the hither and yon of my body, and this sudden outburst of *West Side Story*. They seemed deeply gratified, not just for the performance, but because their medical suspicion about me was now confirmed and, if I couldn't be known to them by name, at least I could be understood in terms of a condition.

Fat lot of good it did me. By the time the surprise had worn off and I was resting comfortably again, no less than six different people had stopped by. The funny thing was, the more they tried to see me, the more invisible I became. It was not my intention. I already said that fooling people is never intentional but that, with the wasties, must be seen as a by-product of the distrust the world places in you—a sort of inverted Cartesianism where all doubt originates outside the thinking ego. Not *Cogito, ergo sum*; but *they* think, therefore I am not.

I repeated the song between cat naps and lapses of euphoria. It came out sounding a little better each time. Words can't describe the thrill I felt each time I belted it out. *Taareeeessssaaaa! Taareeeessssaaaa! I just met a girl named Taareeeessssaaaa!* Until the curtain was called down by a cranky old woman with chest pains stretched out on the gurney just across the corridor. "It's Maria, damn it! Maria! Now would you mind shutting up?"

Maria? Who the hell was Maria? I didn't know any Marias. For a long time everything went dark. I flitted through the pages of my incomplete diary to try and discover the source of the name. But it wasn't there. The closest I got was Theresa, and the moment that happened, my euphoria vanished, and all I could do was weep.

"For the love of Christ," came the voice of the crone, "Now what?" and she asked to be moved.

The nurse promised to do what she could, gave me a once-over that included feeling my pulse, checking the drip on my IV, asking if I could hear her, and, finally, telling me that everything was okay, everything would be alright. I wanted to explain that I wasn't sad because the old bag had told me to shut up. I was sad because I missed Theresa. But when the whole world is fooled, the simplest confusion becomes an ineffable morass and there's nothing you can do but let yourself sink into it.

Eventually, you learn how to have fun. I don't mean in the metaphoric sense, I mean concretely, in the form of lies. Big whopping things that frighten people and make them scurry around looking beneath the surface of everything you say for clues they'll never find. I don't mean fooling. I have already said that, with the wasties, fooling is uninten- tional, is all bound up with clowning and tricks, joking and acting frivolously, with the aim of forgiveness and being excused to the core of your ridiculous nature. The distinc- tion between fooling and lying is an important one. I'm only now beginning to understand how, unlike fooling, lying con- tributes to the development of character. The learning curve is steep. In my own case, I'd say the nearly vertical ascent began when Bond demanded to know why I'd thrown my cup at him.

They all wanted to know.

"Just what is the matter with you?" Gina demanded.

Bond, rubbing the back of his head, scowled his interest in getting an answer.

I glanced at the three of them. They loomed over me, auguries of fearsome punishments. There is a direct correlation between motive and degree of invisibility. The more transparent the motive, the more transparent the lie and vice versa. Thus, when outright denial is impossible, the most effective response is to deny any and all knowledge of motives.

I shrugged.

"You don't know?" Gina asked.

I nodded.

"What do you mean, you don't know?"

Another shrug.

Bond fixed a look on me that took every ounce of insouciance to refract. The more unconcerned I became, the less vigorous his irritation until, finally, he turned away. "Forget it. Never mind." And he signaled Theresa his wish to leave.

The unintended consequence of both my act and my lie was that Theresa left without a good-bye kiss. Not even a hug! All I got was a tentative wave and promises to keep in touch and maybe one day come and visit me at Knickerbocker Estates. Gina herded them out the door, apologizing to Bond for the bump on his head and thanking Theresa for all her hard work and the walkie-talkies and everything she had done for me. And I watched her leave without even a hug or a kiss! She just left.

Forever and ever.

Just like that.

I threw myself into the furthest corner if the sofa, buried my head in my arms, sobbing to the best of my ability and straining straining straining to listen for an interruption in the leave-taking that would mean Theresa was on her way back over to kiss and hug me. After what seemed an eternity of not seeing, I lifted my head up to peek. And Gina caught me.

"That was a pretty lousy good-bye," she said.

I buried my head, kicked once, twice.

"You have no right to feel sorry for yourself," she chided. "No right at all." She collected the wine glasses, carried the tray into the kitchen. "You can't treat people like that and expect them to stick around for long." Then came a crash and Gina's voice. "Oh damn! Damn damn damn! Mike! I need your help!"

I perked up, waited for some sort of refrain—not more broken glass necessarily, though the sound is delightful as a reminder of the fragility of things and the perilousness of present time. With the wasties, about the only thing more delightful than the sound of glass shattering is the sound of a cry for help; and when Gina called again—"Mike! Can you hear me? I need help!"—I struggled to the rescue with every ounce of tender-footed eagerness at my disposal because even the most wasted Boy Scout understands that helping is the surest way of getting from sometimes and maybe to full-time and permanent belonging.

I tumbled from the sofa and scrambled to the kitchen on all fours.

"I'm barefoot," Gina said, pointing to the ground. She was surrounded by shattered wine glasses which, from ground level, gave the impression of a vast, sparkling mine-field. I paused in the doorway. Gina was holding on to the counter for support. "I can't get to the broom," she said. "It's over there." She pointed to the broom closet in the far corner of the kitchen, then began to map a route through the debris by probing with first one foot, then the other, keeping her grip on the counter for balance. "Shoes, Mike. I need my shoes."

I couldn't make out exactly what she wanted and sat

back on my haunches, palms squeezed between my knees. The glass on the floor construed itself into readable, tea leaf–like patterns that shifted in my vision.

"Mike? Did you hear me?"

Very gradually, the first glimpses of what was expected began to crystallize out of the solution, and all my misconducts began to flash before my eyes, every offense from trivial to grave. I began to feel uneasy.

"Mike? Mike!"

I looked up.

"Would you mind?"

I couldn't take my eyes from her, could not see what was required of me.

"Get me my shoes, goddamn it!"

Suddenly, all was clear. Gina needed shoes. And I needed expiation. I crawled into the living room, delirious with fear.

"They're on the mat by the door," came Gina's voice.

Obediently, I plodded on. When I found the shoes I could not figure out how to carry and crawl until her voice rang out, "Did you find them?" and I managed, at last, to clench them in my teeth. This was not the friendly kind of helping I had envisioned. I struggled to keep the shoes in my mouth, laying my ears back, shaggy tail hanging limply behind me like all the dogs of Purgatory—where there are no fetching games, no give-and-take, no acts of courage or valor, but only needs close at hand chasing wants at a distance. I tried to conjure alternative economies of exchange based neither in want or need but just as neat and equable, something mutual and fair and devoid of all the mortifications that go with trying to keep both your dignity and your lover.

But I couldn't. All I could see was Gina stranded in a glittering sea of unhappy inconvenience and hear her cries of "No! Mike! Wait! Stop! Oh, my God! No! Don't," as I struggled to earn her forgiveness across a length of kitchen floor.

I don't understand why my singing career didn't begin then and there. The more I think about it, the less I understand. It just never occurred to me, that's all. It's most likely that Catholic anguish impeded what might have been a straightforward appeal for sympathy, and instead of heroic mortification I could have, say, kissed Gina's feet, begged her forgiveness and sung her a few tunes from *Exile On Main Street* or the Beatles' *White Album*.

No matter. The privilege of my vantage point permits all sorts of explanations, so I'm fairly certain it was no accident. Even as Gina tweezed the glass from my knee and put a Band-Aid on it, I understood that I had achieved a certain beatitude in her eyes. It helped enormously; and when she later told the now ever-present Julian about what I had done, the man went all limp with high-brow compassion, and gave me a volume of his latest translations of Petrarch. I had no clue what he meant by the gift at the time. I no longer gave a shit about the Italian Academy of Advanced Studies in America, or sonnets and canzone or any of the early Renaissance tensions I vaguely remembered him to be involved in. The only thing I wanted was to get my hands on some of his cigarettes. Not to further my depravity or extend my mortifications, but as a satisfying way of embracing finitude and marking time.

. . . which is exactly what I was doing on the gurney in Bellevue: embracing finitude, marking time. Soon after Nurse Moore and the doctors interpreted my condition, I was wheeled into the semiprivacy of a room and installed there behind a drawn curtain. Nurse Moore held my hand

and asked if I might try to sing to her, but what she meant by that I could not figure out.

"Could you sing me your name?"

My name? Exactly how was I supposed to go about that? Before I even had a chance to arrange my facial muscles into an expression of inquiry, she sang, "*Do re mi fa so la ti do.* Can you try it? Come on. Sing with me." And she sang the scale again in a very matronly mezzo-soprano that brought to mind things she'd said about love, calling it benign dementia and saying it should always be without affectation. I agreed with her, and liked her for it. I liked her baggy, night-shift eyes and the way she held my hand, singing *do re me,* not to impress or curry favor or boast of her popularity among cosmopolitans and graduates, but merely to set my angular, professorial mind upon the sinewy track of her poetic example. An explosive rush of euphoria washed over me and, after a minute or two, I heard myself *do re me*-ing right along with her.

"That's wonderful!" she exclaimed; and after several more trips up the scale she put the question to me once again, note for note with *do re me.* "*Now-could-you-please-tell-me-your-name?*"

I waited for an answer, but couldn't come up with anything in the key of C, or any other major mode, for that matter. She squeezed my hand and repeated herself, same notes, same scale; until, at last, my diaphragm began to swell with guitar, bass and drums and in a quavering, nasal drone I began to sing, "*Please allow me to introduce myself . . .*"

Nurse Moore's eyes widened in astonishment. I struggled to get past those two lines and failed. She coaxed and coaxed, repeating her *do re me* over and over; and I don't know if it was because she didn't like the Rolling Stones or if she just liked the Beatles better, because she started singing *"We all live in a Yellow Submarine,"* clapping her hands to the beat and substituting different lyrics. *"Can-you-talk-to-the-song-the-way-I-am, song-the-way-I-am, song-the-way-I-am,"* to show me the way.

I couldn't do it. I tried and tried but couldn't. On top of it all, the memory of those old songs began to make me want my old albums back—The Byrds, The Doors, The Mothers, The Stones, The Beatles, The Kinks, The Stooges, The Grateful Dead, The Tops, The Band, The Who. And, of course, *West Side Story* and Bernstein's Broadway music. Nurse Moore broke off to call the doctors as I struggled to enter the Yellow Submarine from *West Side Story. "Taa-reeeessssaaaa! Taareeeessssaaaa!"*

"Theresa?"

"I just met a girl named Taareeeessssaaaa!"

"Is Theresa your wife?" She asked, noticing the ring on my left hand.

I shook my head.

"Do you know a Theresa?"

I nodded, then shook my head.

"Is that a yes?"

I nodded.

"Do you know her last name?"

"I just met a girl named Taareeeessssaaaa!"

"Is that a yes?"

I nodded.

"Try to sing it," she said; and began to tap out time on the railing.

I tried and tried and tried to come in on the count of 1,2,3,4; but all I could feel was the sputter sputter sputter of Sergeant Pepper's Lonely Hearts Club Band failing to come to life, and the clack clack clack of inwardness, isolation and the final rout of all my earthly relationships.

Nurse Moore stopped beating time and sang one last *do re me* just as the doctor entered the room. As she described our episode together, he listened thoughtfully, appraising me as he would any picturesque, eccentric, secluded stone house on 3.20 acres. His interest seemed to increase as she described the updated, eat-in kitchen, the library, the sunny workroom, the swimming pool and tennis court. I closed my eyes, hoping that when I opened them I'd be alone again. For a moment all was quiet. I felt comfortable, removed. When I opened them again the doctor was flipping through a clipboard. He saw that I was watching him, but ignored me until he had scanned every piece of paper. Then he glanced up and said, "If you don't mind, I'd like to examine you." And I closed my eyes as his hands searched out and tried to localize all the hidden sources of corruption, disquiet and disorder flowing through me like crap through a pipe.

Anyone who doubts that each and every one of us here in Knickerbocker Estates is a work of art has only to take the guided tour. Langer is always happy to give it; and there are any number of docents who volunteer their services and are happy to demonstrate their knowledge. Of course, words like ugliness are never used. But that's only to spare our feelings. What they prefer to concentrate on is the analysis of categories and proceed from the old-fashioned premise that a work of art is a process that has been arrested, is hermetically sealed off and blind yet, in its isolation, represents something to and about the outside world.

So come on in! Call me Sugar. Call me Honey. Call me anything you like because works of art are windowless monads and lead to the universal by virtue of being individuated, singular, and particular—even though, according to the doctors here, basket cases should not be ontologized because each one is unique, and should be studied, though not with the intention of drawing up absolute laws, but to see how each one responds to a program of medication.

We have name plates on our doors, just like in a regular art museum, except the dates of de-composition are left off,

165

as are the names of donors, benefactors and insurance companies. Because of the constantly revised opinions of medical science, no mention is made of media, either. That's why, shortly after my arrival at Knickerbocker Estates, I began a labeling project, not to replace cigarettes in the transcendental unity of my apperception, but so that visitors could see what each work involves, the actual materials. In my own case, for example, it's oil and pastel with an applique of sea grass and Kierkegaard to help in the reconstruction of a thinking ego that has lost all faith and sense of moral duty. All of which is implied in the title I have given to myself: *The Wasties.*

I have been working to label the entire collection here, a job which I'll probably never come to the end of. My goal is to one day have each installation titled and described, not merely for the sake of providing labels, but as an additional step in the accession and cataloging process, so that visitors and researchers alike can have something more to go on than charts and files kept by the doctors, and the kind encouragements of therapists, nurses and visiting families.

My bath toys came in the mail with a letter from Gina and a picture of the nursery she installed in what used to be my bedroom. All traces of me were gone. The room was painted powder blue and furnished with children's decor sprung from the hypoallergenic loins of the age, a place where all the toys are of tasteful wood, and all the rattles sterling, and hanging on the walls are pictures of farms and glades and springtime meadows.

```
Dear Mike,
I wanted you to see how nicely everything
turned out. I'm all ready. My bag is
packed and everything is in place. There
```

is nothing left to do now but wait. Julian
has been an incredible help. He agreed to
be on call when and if I need help getting
to the birthing center. Without you here,
I'm not sure what I will want to do. I
don't feel close enough to anyone else
and asking if he'd be available just in
case seemed sensible. I hope you'll understand and not feel threatened or left out.
It would mean everything to me. By the
time you get this I will have passed my
due date. I'll call you as soon as the
baby arrives.
Love, Gina

I was arranging and rearranging my new toys as H.R.
read me that letter. When he finished, he handed it to me,
pushed his glasses up his nose and waited for a reaction.
The expression on his face was straight out of a physician's
handbook, and intended to inspire something between con-
fidence and intimacy without actually encroaching on
either. Something about the way he had fixed me in his
sights kept me fastened to my chair, something to do with
being an object of sympathy, and understanding the disad-
vantages such attentions put you at. A commotion began in
the corridor just outside my door. H.R. ignored it and pulled
up a chair, holding Gina's letter as if it might grow wings
and fly away.

"Do you understand?" he asked.

I typed my question, printed it on a label for him to wear.

WHAT DO YOU DO WHEN YOU'RE DOWN
TO YOUR LAST MATCH?

H.R. considered my question, and put the letter aside. "I don't know," he said, his face holding its own against his mind's uncertain judgment. It was the first true union between Inner and Outer I'd ever seen in him, and probably something he hasn't had pointed out since his mother caught him stealing glances at her and closed the door on him for the first time in his life. "Light a candle?"

I shook my head.

"Wait for the wind to die down?"

I shook my head.

"Make sure you have plenty of dry wood?"

I shook my head, enjoying the game now and eager to keep it going.

"I give up."

I shook my head.

"No. I mean, tell me," he said, not realizing how close he'd just come to the answer. I wanted to kiss him, shoved the toys off my lap and lunged forward. He stood up, startled, and I fell to the floor at his feet. "What's wrong?" he asked. "Are you alright?" He helped me up. "What was that all about?" An uncertain smile had crept across his face. As I settled back into my Laz-E-Boy, he checked his watch. "It's about time for me to go. Can I get you anything?"

I shook my head.

He put Gina's letter on my writing table, pausing for a moment to look at the view from the window. The mountains were spread in late autumn outline across the horizon. It was a bright, crisp Knickerbocker morning and although there was no snow on the ground, the sunlight dazzled and blinded. "It's a beautiful day," he said at last. "You should try to get outside for some fresh air."

But I had stopped relying on matches long ago, so I didn't.

The Wasties

. . .

Every journey begins and ends with a reorientation. Doctors tend to focus on the cardinal estrangements of person, place and time—at least that was my impression when the Bellevue doctor began his examination with what he very politely described as a brief review. His questions were of the yes/no, rather than the either/or kind, and required nothing more from me than a nod or a shake.

"Can you hear me?"

A nod.

"Can you see me?"

A nod.

"Can you speak?"

"Can you speak?" the doctor asked again.

What was I supposed to say? Yes, Doctor. I have always made my home in language. I'm regular semiotic encyclopedia, as a matter of fact. But from the way he continued to look at me, I could tell he had no semiotics in him; and he moved on to the next question, hustling along as if to capture me in perjury. I tried to whistle up a little euphoria, get some wind into the sails of the mood swelling up inside. But he just touched my shoulder and pressed me back down onto the gurney. "It's alright. Just relax." When I opened my eyes he said, "Shall we continue?"

I blinked, but failed to achieve full visibility. I blinked and blinked and blinked and continued blinking until, gradually, the atmosphere in the room began to coalesce into a full-blown Weltanschauung and a pattern of ideas began to emerge, all begging, just begging to be accepted. There was a telephone on the wall. I wanted to ask the doctor if an outside line could be made available, and maybe getting a pizza or some Chinese food delivered because, suddenly, I was famished.

"Can you write?"

I nodded.

The gurney was cranked until I was sitting up like a spoiled prince. He placed a clipboard in my lap and a pencil in my hand. "Can you write your name for me?"

I had to think about it. I'd been called so many things, was acutely aware of my status as fallen son, not in the military sense of dying for my country or in the biblical sense of repentant wastrel, but in the sense of a lapsed fellowship with my cultivated nature. Caruso was the first name that came to mind; and now that I had proven I could sing, it also felt somehow more real than anything else I could be called.

Caruso

"Caruso? Is that your name?"

Michael

"Michael Caruso?"

I shook my head.

Taylor

"Taylor Caruso?"

I shook my head.

"Michael Taylor Caruso? Is that your name?"

PhD

"Caruso Michael Taylor?"

I shook my head.

PhD

"Excuse me. Dr. Caruso Michael Taylor? Is that your name?"

I shook my head.

The doctor hid his impatience by hiding all signs of it.

"I don't understand," he said, and placed a clean sheet of paper on the clipboard. "Would you please write your name for me? Your legal name?" He pointed to the board. His expression was serious, a man petrified by a superabundance of learning, paralyzed by his own formal powers and an exhausted spirituality. I began to feel sorry for him, then realized that fear, not pity, was the proper response. He seemed so professionally bored that I did not want to answer for fear that I might end up just like him. Besides, you're not supposed to tell strangers your name. You're supposed to get away from them. Run! Hide! And when you're back home, safe and sound, you don't tell your parents about playing outside the neighborhood. You keep it a secret, and continue all the while to yearn for new toys and then, when you grow up, seek liberation from all vanities of passion and the dark cavern of greed. Tears began welling up. I squeezed my eyes shut and felt them spilling down my cheeks. I wasn't sad. I was frightened.

"Are you alright?" the doctor asked. He produced a tissue and offered it to me. "How about another question? What city are we in?"

This was no trick question. I fumbled with the tissue, thinking of Theresa and how she had understood the dainty little joke and grasped my predicament from the moment we first met by agreeing to call me Caruso. I dabbed my eyes and scribbled the answer as promptly as my unsteady hand would allow. It put me in mind of Dr. Eremita, whose questions were never pointed but, rather, edged for hewing, and the answers I provided were sifted through for meaning rather than stacked up against me. So I met the question head on, but the doctor gave no sign of pleasure over the phrases I chose to signal my knowledge of this city of orgies,

171

superb-faced Manhattan, and to demonstrate my robust love for the place, my devotion to its million-footed inhabitants past, present, and future, kissing me ever on the lips and offering me love. Evidently, he did not like being called Camerado, either; and did not know his Whitman. He regarded me with growing mistrust and suspicion, followed up by asking what time it was, not realizing that I had no use for time, and therefore no means of keeping it. I pointed to my wrist, then to his. He extended his arm, allowing me to read the time from his watch. The sight of that beautiful golden thing sent a rush of envy through me. A Rolex Navigator!

Can I have it?

The doctor ignored the question, retracted his arm and retreated into the next question. "Was it daytime or nighttime when you came here?"

I'll be your best friend!

That ended the questions. For the next few minutes he pushed, squeezed and tapped me, he shined his light in my eyes and ears. Then he left. That was it.

Corazon Aquino came in afterwards to clean me up. I hadn't understood why everybody was shying away from me; but when Ms. Aquino removed my diaper it was clear that I was responsible for stinking up all of Bellevue. I became embarrassed and felt unworthy, but Ms. Aquino showed absolutely no sign of distaste or disgust and I immediately understood how she had risen to power after the assassination of her husband. It wasn't just her stoicism and commitment to duty, but the way she cleansed me, as if restoring me to a state of moral perfection and emotional equilibrium were her only care in the world. I wanted to ask her about People Power and her problems with the generals, Ferdinand and Imelda Marcos, the CIA; but she was clearly very much in demand and had to leave, drawing the curtain around me as she departed. In her wake I found a new insight into the nature of politics as a form of nursing. After all, if the goal of politics is to maintain the inner teleology of the state in order to ensure the viability of its institutions over time, then at its noblest core the process is much the same as changing diapers and easing discomfort, bed by stinking bed.

It took some time to get used to the new diaper she'd put me in, the unfamiliar symmetries of its different folds and chafe lines. I had just closed my eyes when the curtain was yanked aside. "Rise and shine Dolly Pops! I'm taking you upstairs!"

I blinked, tried to rub my eyes, but was stopped short by the wafting fragrances of aftershave and the straps that had been laid across me as I slept. Ishmael? Was it Ishmael Reed?

"That's right buddy old pal. We're going up. Double the pleasure double the fun. The neurology service wants *you*! Soon as I get you unhooked here."

I recognized the antic syntax of his neo-Hoodoo dialect, and wanted to tell him I'd been a long-time admirer of his verse and once heard him read years ago at a colloquium and wanted to ask how it happened that this particular hospital came to be staffed by African American literary icons and Third World Revolutionaries. Was it part of a wider plan? Or just another painful irony in the legacy of racism—a sick society tended to by its own oppressed. He didn't speak as he fussed with the straps and levers. I tried to prop myself up, wishing I could tell him that I was with him all the way—and not just as another guilt-ridden,

Unknown White Male, which is what the bracelet on my wrist said, or some idiot pandering to an ideology of liberation as existential padding for an otherwise empty life—but with him in the transcendental sense of united natures and trans-generational time.

As he wheeled me down the corridor I began to recognize many of the other greats who worked here on behalf of Unknown White Male suffering. I saw Gwendolyn Brooks, June Jordan, Rita Dove, Langston Hughes, Richard Wright—all the greats, interns, residents volunteers from twentieth-century struggles all around the globe. There was W. E. B. Du Bois and Patrice Lumumba going over a patient's chart, Antonio Gramsci and Ho Chi Minh making their respective ways to Nuclear Medicine. I saw Che Guevara, Eugene V. Debs, Mother Teresa, Mahatma Gandhi, Emiliano Zapata, Leon Trotsky, Albert Schweitzer, groups of East Timorese, Philippinos, and an assortment of South American magical realists. Then, don't ask me how, but we got into an elevator with Mikhail Bulgakov, who whistled the tune to *He's the Man Who Broke the Bank at Monte Carlo* all the way up to the eighth floor.

I can't say exactly what the next sequence of events entailed, but there was plenty of cross-talk, hip-hop, exchanges of documentary and vital information; a short, tightly scripted whirl that flew past me and left me trying to fathom how, when, and why I had come to find myself in a room with seven other beds looking out a window at the East River and the Queensboro Bridge, overwhelmed by the austere benevolence of Bellevue's Neurology Service.

It was singing that had got me there and singing that would get me out. My fellow patients weren't exactly thrilled. They hated it, yelled at me to shut up. The staff warned me several times to keep it down or else. But what alternative did I have? It was sing or sink.

Although my vocal chords had gone slightly to rust, the mere use of them, combined with the view from the window of the Queensboro Bridge, sent thrilling shivers of *dooten doo doo* straight through me. Some claim I mumbled for a solid hour, but without Art Garfunkel to harmonize with what more did they want? A goddamn Central Park reunion? And anyway, *Badaba die die die die, feelin' groovy* and *dooten doo doo, feelin' groovy* produce totally different euphoric effects. The former is based in eschatology (die die die die), while the other is purely scatological (doo doo). When you think about it, an Iron Age suspension bridge over the East River is as good an object of contemplation as any; and singing *dooten doo doo* or *badaba die die die die—* I shit, I die, I feel groovy—is no different than *ham sa ham sa* in as far as both lead to groovy feelings and higher consciousness. Furthermore, in my opinion, the view of the 59th Street bridge adds a contemporary relevance to the mantra that is completely lost in the Sanskrit.

My first visitor after the Jell-O cup and oatmeal breakfast introduced himself as a social worker, but I wasn't fooled. I knew who he was immediately, and figured that the deception was merely a polite way of putting me at ease with his slightly different vision of America, one inspired by the other bridge, the Brooklyn Bridge. He wanted to know if I had a home and a family. When I nodded affirmative, he seemed pleased and relieved. He asked some other questions, too, but I was more interested in discussing the amazing coincidence that had brought us together under the shadows of two completely different bridges and visions of the future—his Brooklyn Bridge, sleepless, vaulting over seas and prairies, uniting the continent; and Simon and Garfunkel's 59th Street Bridge, which sends you dappled and drowsy and ready to sleep into a dreamland of private euphoria.

When he asked me what I was singing, I hardly knew what to say. Then I realized, of course! Hart Crane couldn't have known the Simon and Garfunkel song. On top of that, he would have been completely unfamiliar with grooviness except, perhaps, in the sense of a strident freedom of spirit—which goes far deeper than the 1960s' connotation of sensual stimulation and pleasure. I wanted to let him know that I was as attuned to his sensibility as I was affected by Simon and Garfunkel—and T. S. Eliot, too, for that matter. I wanted to explain that I appreciated him, and saw nothing but the grossest irony in the fact that his ecstatic affirmation of the human spirit had forced him to jump off a ship, whereas the author of *The Waste Land* lived long and comfortably with his dark vision. By the way, it was during this interview with Hart Crane that I coined the term wasties: Waste + ies, plural variant of the suffix *y,* a form of the familiar diminutive, meaning "Small one" or "Dear one"—an unlikely-sounding noun with fuzzy adjectival overtones; in short, a nonce word to depict a condition that is a product both of culture and biology. "The Wasties" borrows from T. S. Eliot and Simon and Garfunkel inasmuch as it connotes both darkness and grooviness, establishes links between all that is cruel, forbidding and falling down (London Bridge for Mr. Eliot, a naturalized Anglophile) and all that is joyful, spontaneous, and beyond all urges. In addition, each has its own bridge as a point of reference; all thanks to Crane, who seemed amused to hear me *dooten doo doo-ing,* but not enough to recommend that

I be transferred to a homeless shelter upon my release from neurology.

"I'm going to wait until after the psychiatric evaluation," he said in a manner which I understood was meant to reassure. "Meanwhile, I've been going through the phone book. You wouldn't believe how many Taylors there are in this city. That is your name, isn't it? Taylor?"

I nodded.

"Good." He patted my knee. "Now you get some rest while I get to work on it."

Knickerbocker Estates resembles Europe during the late Middle Ages because all who enter its confines find themselves living under a common veil of half-consciousness and entrust their humanity to therapists, care-givers and medication like so many popes and princes entrusted their humanity to sorcerers, priests and witches. But if Knickerbocker Estates resembles medieval Europe, assisted living itself is more like Rome or Athens, cities which continue to thrive as ruins. You can look at their monuments and reliquaries, get stuck in traffic, pickpocketed, have a bad meal in a good restaurant and a good meal in a bad restaurant, all in the same day. Assisted living retains all of the essential elements of life in an ancient capital, a place that thrives on seediness and continual reseeding, and has held both processes in unique balance for long enough to become a source of worry and tourist revenue. I don't mean to imply that assisted living goes on atop treasures and a fantastic history buried beneath the pavement, but merely that, like these great ancient cities, the past is as much an encumbrance and a burden as it is a source of pride and wonderment. Which, of course, is precisely why you have to leave the Acropolis alone, and the Coliseum and the Pyramids and the Great Wall and Stonehenge—because in assisted living, you never accomplish anything, but only live in earnest need to. You try to cook for yourself, and crap without soiling your diaper, and call upon the angels and demons of your entire ancestry for cues. You try to re-erect all the monuments, put in new roads and infrastructure, gird yourself for anticipated growth and restore quaint old services like milk delivery, passenger ships, afternoon newspapers, and the soul's relationship to the body—if not an exact correlation between Inner and Outer, then at least a passable resemblance—so you can answer Whitman's three questions: Who are you elderly man so gaunt and grim with well grey'd hair and flesh all sunken about the eyes? Who are you sweet boy with cheeks yet blooming? Who are you my dear comrade?

Word of my singing got around quickly. It was one of the first things I was asked to do when I arrived at Knickerbocker Estates. I declined from day one, because who wants to admit that the collected work of one's entire being is floating in a sea of old Broadway tunes and hits from the '50s, '60s and '70s? It's rock 'n' roll all the way down, I'm embarrassed to admit. But is it my fault that I've been left with little more to work with than this famishing pabulum of hits, and a vocational vocabulary that, when you put them together, make your world seem neither half-full nor half-empty but exactly half-necessary?

When H.R. finds me at my desk laboring away at my labels, he always asks permission before taking a book from the shelf to read to me aloud. Then, he generally asks to see what I've been working on, so I print out a sample from the most recent batch for him to read. I'm not sure what he derives from all this beyond a certain care-giverly pleasure that he intends as groundwork for establishing a therapeutic relationship. He is fascinated with all the gifts from Gina and Julian Bloom, particularly the paperback I wrote, which he treats with great respect, as if it were a smoking gun, evidence of a formerly fully ontologized being. I am tired of all the clue finding, tired of the woes they induce, tired of the questions they inspire. Part of it is my own fault, I'm sure. Not in the sense that I present H.R. with an enigma, but in the sense that all who visit me seem to believe my essential nature is somehow contained in the surrounding artifacts—my toys, my presents, my notes and, most importantly, my labels. I have put a new label on my front door, but it's not having the intended effect. It says *NO ASSEMBLY REQUIRED*. How much more painfully can I put it? I might as well never have posted it. H.R. and all the rest of them ignore it completely, come bounding in here with this that and the other, gather their tit-bits, scurry off to put them together according to the latest instruction manual, which just gets thicker and thicker with every newly collected piece of evidence.

It was H.R. who finally got me to join the daily Knicker-bocker Estates nature walk. It was partially the way he read to me, standing next to my window silhouetted by morning light, and partially the aftereffect of a sleepless night during which I tried and tried and tried to orient myself in relation to ebbing memory and the me this flow of words has become. I wasn't anticipating any Great Awakening, or trying to stimulate myself in the direction of what is called "self-fulfillment," because, for one thing, I was already too wide awake for comfort and, for another, the wasties affirms

179

emptiness as the only possible outcome of self-fulfillment. Once the incomprehensible monster at your core has been slain and the mysteries of the self dragged into the light—there's not much of interest left to do except worry about your looks. In the end, the only fulfillment one can hope for is to carry the integrity of childhood along into old age, the integrity that comes with innocence, and makes us want to become firemen, ballerinas, astronauts, sailors, teachers, raccoons and dogs when we grow up.

I was tired when H.R. took my blood pressure. I was tired of the daily basket of pills I needed and the zinc oxide ointment, and all the random invasions my semiprivacy invited. I was tired of the view across the Hudson, the whirr of my IBM ThinkPad, and printer, and label after label after label, herewith the most recent (my next-door neighbor):

INCREDIBLE ODDS. CA. 1948
MEDIA: ASPHALT DRIVEWAY WITH APPLIQUES OF
GREY HAIR, EZ PASS, ERGONOMIC OFFICE
FURNITURE, GRILLED
VELVEETA CHEESE SANDWICH, SWIMMING POOL,
SOFTBALL GLOVE

Gina's letter was still on the desk. H.R. pretended not to notice it when he reached for the book, thumbed it in his usual manner of seeming preoccupied with the vaguest recollection of his Universidad days, but, in fact, honing in on precisely the verse to suit the moment. Did I mention that H.R. was Mexican and devoutly Catholic and thus more attuned to the Petrarchan lyric than we prose-addled Anglo-Saxon dictaphones? He reminded me of Theresa, and there were times when I wished he'd mention Neruda just to complete the synonymy. But he never did, and I didn't ask, for fear I wouldn't understand the consequences and only come to resent Mr. Langer and the other silver-haired, charismatic mega-vertebrates who had lured him here with substandard benefits and below-market wages.

So H.R. read to me. *A qualunque animale alberga in terra / Se non se alquanti c'hanno in odio il sole,* which translated goes: *To animals that live on earth / Except those few that hate the sun.* He went on for what seemed ever about hiding in the forest and weeping in wonder at the cruel stars above and letting my body rot in the ground, and it dawned on me that he was telling me I had better get outside and play or lose the chance forever. The metaphysics of it all was lost on me, but the thoughtful air he put on and the way he rubbed his chin made me see how being locked up inside a house in a forest was exactly what every kid feared more than anything. Suddenly, I was up and rummaging underneath my bed for the walkie-talkies.

"What's this?" H.R. asked as I held one out for him to take. "Radios?"

I nodded and pointed outside. A few minutes later we were stalking toward a bench at the far edge of the big lawn. It was a favorite of many assisted-livers because of the view and because it marked the entrance to a path that led down to the river, the sort of place where childhoods begin and end. You could follow the path down, learning the names of plants and animals along the way, or skip stones and hoot at the big boats churning up- and downriver; you could go birding or take a whizz against a tree, look for wild mushrooms or Indian trails, propose a hike or cop a feel. Or you could just sit on the bench up top and take in the view with no intention of ever enrolling in it—which is what I chose to do, not because I was afraid of wild nature but because I didn't want to lose my boyhood in it.

"I have to go," H.R. said. "But I'll keep this. Call me when you're ready to come back." He clicked his transmit button twice to demonstrate. "It was a good idea to bring these. I'm going to mention it at the next staff meeting. Maybe we can get some for the others to use." He patted me on the shoulder and strolled away.

It was good to be outside. I don't know how many days or weeks had passed since I became an assisted-liver, but as I sat there they peeled off me like dead skin. My first instinct was to compose a label, something involving the Hudson River School, not *Voyage of Life* or *Course of Empire* or *River in the Catskills,* but just a pen and pencil cloud study with numbers for colors and notes about the effect on landscapes of rain, mountains, plastic bags, Mylar balloons, geological time and Darwin. But the longer I sat there, the less inclined I became to depict the view for fear of becoming entrapped in it. I gripped the edge of the wooden bench for support as a squall blew up and began to toss me among the psalms and sonnets of the ocean I was lost upon. I felt my vocal chords begin to flutter and, rather than swallow hard and refuse the request, which had been my reaction since coming to Knickerbocker Estates, I unfurled them and allowed them to take the breeze. What came out had less to do with the view of the mountains across the river than it did with the idea that I was alone on a precipice and nobody could hear me. I can't say exactly what came out, but I recognized shards and snippets and bits and pieces and pops and scratches of every poem and song I'd ever learned in school over years and years of reading and writing and striding among my peers. The experience was not at all unpleasant. As a matter of fact, it sustained my euphoria for longer than I feel comfortable admitting, kept me surging with all the pleasures of multiple orgasm, and would only that I could have achieved and maintained an erection, I'd have covered the entire hillside with a lava flow of semen right down to where it joined the mighty Hudson.

I heard a voice.

"Professor Taylor."

I clutched the rim of the bench. The cloud studies cleared from view, along with echoes of numbered colors and songs and the distant mountains. I remember thinking how funny the term "brain event" sounded when I first heard that I'd hosted one. The first thought that had come to me was of being a passenger in a crashing Boeing 747. But that had been all wrong. If there's anything more that can be said about the wasties than I've already said, it would have to be that every day is an interpretive act that you aspire anew and anew and anew to. There was nothing to distract me from that perfect spot I'd found on the bench, not even the idea that laughter is the highest, truest expression of pessimism because it is both the *only* proof that the world is not entirely miserable, and the *only* way to make the best of it. In the end, all you can be certain of are your numbered days and all the poems, prayers, and hit songs you can remember.

"Professor Taylor. Come in, Professor Taylor."

I glanced at the Motorola beside me on the bench and realized it meant me.

"Professor Taylor. Click once if you can hear me. Over."

I picked up the little radio, thrilled to hear it working so conveniently and well across all those yards and yards of vacant space. I pressed the button as requested, and something impelled me to hold it and something else impelled me to try and sing "Blowin' in the Wind"—but I only got as far as *How many roads* when my finger slipped from the button and H.R.'s excited voice crackled back at me. "Your wife, Professor Taylor. I'm coming to get you!"

You won't believe it, but guess what!

?

No, guess!

?

Oh, come on. Try.

. . .

You don't want to or you can't? Don't tell me. It's because you don't want to play. That's it. You don't want to play with me. Well, okay. Fine. But you'll be sorry. Believe me, you'll be sorry. And don't come crying back to me later, begging to guess, because it will be too late. So fuck off. Fuck guessing. Fuck being and thinking, *Dichtung und Denken.* Fuck the whole, the original whole and the whole of which we are but a fragment of an image. Fuck me and you and everything that follows. Fuck human history and the history of that history. Fuck content and context. Fuck nature. Fuck culture. Fuck theory of all kinds and fuck the flowing rivers.

So. I'll give you one more chance. Want to guess?

. . .

No? Okay then. I'll tell you. *It's a boy!*

That's right. A boy! Want to guess how I know? Forget it. I'll tell you anyway. Gina told me. On the phone.

"Mike? Mike? It's a boy, Mike. Can you hear me? It's a boy!"

I was nodding and H.R. leaned into the mouthpiece. "He hears you, Mrs. Taylor. He's smiling."

"He's beautiful, Mike." And then it was hard to hear because she just kept cooing he's beautiful, he's just so beautiful, into the phone.

H.R. took the receiver from me and said, "We'll call back in a little while, okay? Maybe you can write something on the computer and I'll read it to her." He made the same suggestion to Gina and, with his arms across my shoulder, we made our way to the Laz-E-Boy so I could sit down. "Eight pounds, six ounces. That's a healthy boy," H.R. said. He patted my shoulder. "A very good size. Congratulations!" He beamed so wide his mustache nearly slipped right off his face. I wanted to laugh and be happy, but all I could think of were flowers. All sorts of flowers. Don't ask me why, because I have never given flowers much thought and don't know much of anything about them at all, except in the metaphoric sense of that part of a plant comprising the reproductive organs and their envelopes, the blossom considered independently of the plant which bears it, the best and brightest embodiment of any quality which thrives, is distinguished among others of its class, and falls to seed or is plucked to decorate the monuments of the dead.

I rose up from the Laz-E-Boy and was helped by H.R. to my desk. He watched as I began to type up a new label; but no sooner had I typed in the first word than he leapt into action. "Of course! We must. Right away!" And he picked up the telephone, which in assisted living functions generally as a decoration, since none but the sturdiest can use it—and arranged delivery of a large bouquet. I was distracted by all his expertise and broke off my label-making; but when he saw me gaping at him, he flapped a hand and said, "Go on. Write. Write out a message!"

So I typed up the full text of the label in my head and printed it out. He scanned it, scratched his head, then flashed me a cheek-wrinkling wink. "Love, Mike," he said into the phone. "That's right. Just Mike." Then he hung up and helped me back to the Laz-E-Boy. "Get some rest now. She'll get them in a couple of hours." Then he left me to doze away about lilacs and anemones, primrose and roses and lilies and hyacinths and nicotine—*Nicotiana tabacum,* that is, since it had been time immemorial since I'd last smoked, and yet the vestiges of the thrill still rattled through me like a virulent, brittle nostalgia and put me in mind of Movie Tone newsreels, the 1956 Olympic Games, a haze of retroceding thought-feelings rising up and filling my whole carboy with smoky atmosphere.

There is no dreaming with the wasties, only a process of inner transmutation that takes place in darkness, transpires independently of both conscious and unconscious, yet is also comprehensible and individuated. There is no dreaming because you are your dreaming, and I don't mean in some made-for-TV movie be-all-that-you-can-be way, but in the sense of a creature risen from the depths, consonant with the silence at the center of things. And when I opened my eyes and saw Gina and Julian Bloom standing beside my Bellevue bed conferring with a nurse in whispers, the first thought that went though my head was not

"I'm dreaming;" but "Oh Captain! my Captain, our fearful trip is done!"

She bent toward me. "Mike? Are you awake?"

I couldn't answer honestly so I just allowed myself to gaze into the blue aquatints that are her eyes and give myself over to the euphoria of the New World I discovered there. She leaned closer, kissed my forehead. "Mike. Mike. Mike. Everything's going to be okay. Oh, Mike, Mike, Mike."

Julian appeared at her side, put a hand on her shoulder. He looked upon me as upon a sustained injury. He didn't speak, but said it all.

Gina backed away, produced a tissue, dabbed her eyes and nose. "You just relax," she told me. "We're going to take you home."

Julian glanced toward the other beds in the ward, crumpled his nose. "As soon as the paperwork gets done. Which, in this place, you never know."

I turned to look out the window. It was all clouds and dampness. The bridge was only partially visible. Somebody cut loose a thundering fart which startled my visitors. I laughed, which came out in a series of abrupt stutters. Gina stepped up, pressed her belly against the railing on the bed. "Are you alright? Shall I call the nurse?"

Call the nurse? I felt my diaphragm begin to swell and relax, swell and relax, as the words to the "59th Street Bridge" song passed in front of me. My eyes brimmed with happiness at the sight of my beautiful wife and the joyous cries of my heart and I began to sing *Slow down. You move too fast.* But I had to stop for lack of oxygen before I could get to *You got to make the mornin' last.*

Astonishment. Glances all around.

"Mike?"

"What was that?"

"Mike! You were singing!"

"That was singing?"

Gina's hands were on me, face to face, as a voice from a bed faraway cried out "Nurse! He's doing it again!" And another voice, fainter, less resolute called "Will somebody please tell him to shut up!" Which had the effect of increasing my joy to a nearly combustible level and I belted *All is groovy!*

A nurse appeared and Gina stepped away to let her at me. "There, there," she said. "You're going to have to keep it down, Mr. Taylor. Do you understand?" And she took my wrist to feel my pulse. When she was finished she turned to Gina and Julian.

"Is he alright?"

"It sounds like he's trying to sing," Julian added.

The nurse quickly explained how, yes, I had been singing like this all night, and they weren't able to make out what I was trying to say, either. Gina stepped toward the side of the bed. "That's great! Honey! You're using your voice."

Then Julian piped in, "What do the doctors say?"

"I don't know," the nurse admitted as she adjusted the sheets on the bed and checked the intravenous line going into my arm. "You'll have to wait until Dr. Matthew arrives."

"Mike! You can sing!"

Upon which another thundering fart erupted from somewhere on the ward and I couldn't help but laugh and laugh because, when you come right down to it, the passing of gas is terribly funny, one of the most hilarious things a human being can do in public.

"Does he need a change?" Gina asked.

"I just checked him," the nurse replied. "It's just a little gas."

"Is he laughing?" Julian asked.

The nurse patted me on the knee and said she'd come back a little later. I turned my head to see who had done it but the railing blocked my view. I wanted to congratulate the man, whoever he was; explain that it wasn't the fart itself but the way in which it enters the crowd that I was laughing at; the fact that the greater the noise, the greater the opportunity for personal growth. No matter how vast your consciousness, you stand exposed as a helpless victim of your own bodily functions and, goddamn! There ain't nothin' funnier than the humiliation that goes with admitting *that* piece of evidence in court.

"We're going to get you home just as soon as possible," Gina was telling me as she held my hand. Between occasional strokes of my forehead and asides to Julian, who stood by dutifully, I came to learn exactly how my every wish had been fulfilled and how, in spite of all the terror and angst my disappearance had struck into everyone's heart, all were glad I hadn't been hit by a truck or drowned in the river or mugged and left for dead in the park, but was still alive.

Of course, none was gladder than I to hear how much grief my absence had caused. You never fully enter the world unless you have been missed by someone and you should never, ever, leave it until you have missed someone in return. Love's objects are given and taken away randomly, and whether you were born in a pigsty and never put up for adoption or were cooed over by a beautiful biological mother whose breasts oozed free-range organic milk, and a father who resigned his presidency to take you and your friends camping—or whether, like most, you just stood awkwardly along the wall waiting waiting waiting, or threw yourself into competitive sports or got your genitals pierced for the sheer spontaneity of it all or death-tripped your way through adolescence and into the Bar exam to find yourself fidgeting and fussing with high-end recreation gear on the weekend when you become the superb superhero of all your gorgeous neighbor's dreams—love is all luck luck luck, with doses of self-abuse tossed in here and there, punctuated by moments and glimpses of higher consciousness, transcendence and sainthood. And that's just the cliché part. To get to the quintessence of it all you need scuba gear, and not of the friendly Jacques Cousteau deep-sea sort, but the stuff you find yourself strapped into under protest and much wailing, to be pitched overboard under cover of night and left to drift away among the monsters of the unconscious.

That's the love that I was overcome with when they wheeled me out of the Neurology Service. Aung San Suu Kyi was pushing the wheelchair and talking about the Burmese government in exile and the multinational oil and gas crimes of Unocal and French Total; but I was too involved with my own independence movement to follow up or keep up with what was being said. Gina, being a lawyer, handled all the forms and paperwork beautifully, reading and signing with her belly pressed up against the counter; never flagging, in spite of the high fluorescence, spit-and-shine cinder-block sheen that, she remarked to Julian, made her glad she'd chosen the birthing center over hospital obstetrics, blowing strands of beautiful brown bangs from her face as she signed me out of there.

I don't know how they did it. Suddenly, I wasn't wearing the bracelet that said Unknown White Male but my own, clean clothes, the Modern Language Association T-shirt, olive-green corduroys, beat-up burgundy oxfords and, on my lap, the sport coat Gina bought me as a present when we did those sorts of things for each other. I looked like I was headed for Philosophy Hall, and with Julian Bloom taking over from the Burmese Nobel Peace Laureate to push me the final stretch out to the street, I could have sworn we had all been somehow restored to an earlier variation of things, and practically expected Julian to start talking about medieval allegorizations of Eurydice and the Phoenix myth, while Gina decided where to go for sushi. A swell of joy flowed into me from nowhere and, as we approached the automatic glass doors, beyond which the city's traffic thrummed, I gripped the arm-rests and let the Dylan in me loose with every bit of nasal contralto and twangy guitar. *All I rillyyyy wanna dooooooo is baby make friends with youu- uuu!* Which arrested Julian in mid-stride and caused Gina to stop short, half smiling, half looking for the emergency exits, while I segued through *Oh, mama. Can this really be the end?* And *Oh, sister! When I come to knock on your door* as the big glass entryway hissed, unable to shut or to open any wider. I held on and rocked all I could for Gina and only for Gina and all forms of Gina, stopping only when she dropped into a difficult expectant mother squat beside me, put the flat of her hand on my cheek and said in a sweet whisper, "Shhhh. It's alright. Everything's going to be alright. I'm taking you home." But I knew it was only tem- porary and that, ultimately, she was not referring to that sweet point of stillness above the turning world, our West End Avenue bower, but to Knickerbocker Estates.

In the cab, Julian sat up front, twisting around only to ask if everything was alright when I broke into a little fit of post-euphoric sobbing because I couldn't remember the words to "Shelter from the Storm" or "Lay Lady Lay," though it was exactly what I wanted to thank Gina for giving me and exactly what I most desired to have from her in return. She let me rest my head on her shoulder and I did that for the whole ride uptown, exchanging rear-view glances with the driver, who I gave up trying to place, though he bore a striking resemblance to Rabindranath Tagore in his *Gitanjali* period.

I did not recognize the apartment. Gina assured me we were home and said not to worry, the plastic tarpaulins covering the furniture and floors would be gone as soon as Vinnie and his crew were finished their work. In the meantime, she said, we could sleep in her bedroom. *Her* bedroom! That was what she called what used to be my study, the place she moved into after I started my smoking project. I wanted to know who moved the dresser and the mirror and all the little artifacts of our marriage, including the queen-sized bed, which was too big for the room but not big enough to contain all the piles of paper she brought home from the office. I stood, propped in the doorway, afraid to enter and afraid to leave. I remembered John Muir's last words to me before he stole my wallet. He told me not to mind him and reminded me how such little note is taken of the deeds of nature and said I should consider how nobody reports the works and ways of the clouds in the sky though they come into creation every day like freshly up-heaved mountains—so I should not report him. He said a person needed imagination to comprehend the immortal beauty of Nature, and our bodies were made to thrive only on pure air—so what did I need my wallet for, anyway?

Pure air was exactly what I needed as I surveyed the unmade bed, which Gina began to clear of all her papers. I turned and began to make my way to the old bedroom, but

Gina took my elbow. "It's a mess. There's nothing in there,
Don't worry. It's only for a few more days." She turned me
around and guided me back. Next I knew, we were standing
in front of a mirror. Gina modeled her belly, turning to
either side for profile, running her hand over it like a duly
sated banqueter. She tugged me nearer, pointed to the man
and woman facing out at us. "You need a bath," she said.
"And a shave."

The next thing I knew I was in the tub and Gina was
pouring water over me. She had stripped down to her
underwear and huffed and puffed with pregnant effort as
she washed me. I was impervious to all the fun she tried to
have at my expense, calling me Mountain Man and saying I
smelled like I was homeless and slept on grates. The only
portion of me she left unwashed were my privates, lying
down there at the end of me like an unharvested crop.

Suddenly, I was ashamed. I covered myself with my
hands. Gina glanced at me with a look of mild surprise, and
I think we both suddenly realized we no longer knew each
other, and everything that had ever existed between us was
now reduced to a slow dance of pretty words around inexpressible feelings. It is said that the world is everything that
is the case, and that sounds ecstatic enough, and true—but
what about my measly nuts and the desires that attach to
them, and my beautiful, pregnant wife who used to fall like
aching matter into my arms at the end of the day and now
only appears before me in her underwear, no longer part of
all that is the case but, instead, as deserted from me as the
moon? What about what *was* the case? What world does
that belong to? What belongs in that world? What about the
apartment I no longer recognized or belonged to? What
about my books and friends, my fun and games? What

about the breezes that blew into our windows at night and the talking and laughter that floated off on them? What about my baby teeth? And what my mother thought when they began to fall out? What about my mother and father? All our songs and carols?

She dried me off and took me back into the bedroom where, after drifting for a time as king on the queen-sized Posturepedic, I opened my eyes and heard the water running in the shower. I got up, fumbling, unsteady, hand over foot, leaned in the bathroom doorway and helped myself to a view of her in the shower. I spied through the transparent curtain as she soaped belly and breasts, bathed herself under flowing water. She turned, water flowing down upon her head, and saw that I was watching. For a moment I thought she might change into a deer and flee, or a tree, or an advertisement—or turn modestly and wish me away. But she didn't. Instead, she smiled, looked down upon her transformed, ovoid body, then back at me, and blew a spray of water from her lips, happy to impugn me with my fair portion of responsibility, or guilt, or whatever you care to call the sudden comprehension of our estate, the changing nature of the interests we held in common, and their relation to our rights and the rest of the world. I wanted to root myself, right there in the doorway, turn into a tree or a stone or some other immovable object. But, instead, I became frightened, and stumbled back into the bedroom. It wasn't Gina who was frightening. She was beauty itself. It was her appearance, and the fact that her body governed all relationships, and that from it would issue all the gravestones scattered in our future.

She came to me wrapped in a bath towel, humming just loudly enough to herself for me to see that she was happy.

She talked to me as she dressed, telling me how insane with worry everybody had been. "Vinnie thinks it's all his fault," she mentioned by the by. "He stayed here until two this morning and wanted to come with me to the hospital." She disappeared for several minutes, then returned, freshly dressed.

I settled back among the pillows and closed my eyes again, happy just to hear Gina's shuffling and bustling through the apartment, and desiring nothing else. Happiness is too rude a word to call the state I became suspended in. With the wasties, happiness has nothing to do with raptures of pleasure, enjoyment, satisfaction, the good life. In fact, there is next to nothing of these things that can pertain to the wasted view of happiness, which derives not from feeling at all, but wholly from mattering—not merely to one or another, but to the order of Being, and not as an instance of it, another quaint sideshow linking past and present, grandparent and grandchild, but as part of the infinite regress in the unfolding narrative that holds us in thrall.

I heard her talking on the telephone in the living room, smelled sautéing garlic and onions, felt the reverberations of home all around me. Once or twice, she poked her head into the door, and when she saw that I was still lying on the bed, one eye closed, one eye cocked open to take in all the form-combining possibilities of the walls and ceiling, she ducked back out and resumed her homemaking.

Presently, she was sitting on the side of the bed and I was propped up by a levy of pillows, taking bites of an omelette and watching as she prized another morsel onto the tines of the fork, brought it to my mouth, guarding against spill with cupped hand and talking to me of things I had no clue of and not minding that I was clueless. When the omelette was finished, she wiped my mouth with a napkin, then kissed me on the cheek and sat back for a look at me. I could not fashion or formulate much of a response to the occasion or do much of anything but know we were omnipresent together and immanent. She stood up and brushed invisible crumbs from the bed. Euphoria began to creep up and the beginning of a song without words. She said, "Try to get some sleep now."

When she closed the door, I saw my packed bags waiting, and knew we had arrived at our last day together.

Whoever heard of a museum where the artwork roams around viewing the viewer? That's more or less what assisted living is all about. Not just for me but for all the work in here. With the wasties the distinction between Inner and Outer has been completely eradicated, and you find yourself satisfying and being satisfied by all nine muses at once. This is not to say that the wasties is a state of perfect alignment between art and life; just a greater precision in the use of materials.

I was sitting on my favorite bench casting the river scenery into idealized shapes and forms with hues borrowed from the Hudson River School—Frederick Church, mainly—ocher and yellow twilight, clouds sweeping over a wild stillness punctuated by trees rising up in the foreground as a boundary between way in here and way out there. Gina had called to say she got the flowers and to thank me for the note. I don't know what the note she referred to had said; but I was always happy to listen to the sound of her voice over the telephone.

"I'll describe him to you," she said.

I glanced up at H.R., who was filling up the calendrical pill dispenser, my assisted living book of hours.

"He has this fine brown hair; not as dark as mine but not as light as yours. His lips are so sweet and rosy and perfect. The upper has a cute little dip in it. It's so tiny and delicate. He sort of looks like you around the eyes. Right now the color is this amazing metallic blue. His brows slant down just like yours. And all he wants to do is eat."

I listened but couldn't get beyond the vaguest outline of what she was describing. It was something way beyond a baby; something way, way more. But I was not able to grasp exactly what it was, grew confused and confounded by the variables and functions and parameters and demands of an emotional calculus far beyond my capabilities. Suddenly there was an eruption of wailing and she said, "Sorry, honey. I need to go. I'll call later."

I gave the telephone back to H.R. "Anything wrong?" he asked.

I shook my head. I wasn't crying. I was figuring. I was calculating the value of all the mortal qualities that reside in us when you subtract love, when you disallow it as an aim or an outcome.

"You want me to turn on the radio?"

I nodded, feeling on the verge of great desperation and emptiness, sitting in the big Laz-E-Boy, sleeping off the springtime of my history. H.R. turned on NPR at the same moment that Paulette wheeled in my lunch. She called to me in her singsong warble. "How you doin', Sugar?"

A while later, I made my way out to the bench to watch the Frederick Church sky across the Hudson.

I didn't notice it when the wheelchair arrived and parked beside me. It might have been there the whole time, for all I could remember. The chair was turned with its back toward me; but I didn't need to see any other angle to recognize it as the George Segal I had labeled some days earlier, a frail, middle-aged woman who lived a corridor away and whose head was held up by a metal brace. I continued to look, and began to realize that I had mislabeled her. This was no plaster cast taken from life. This was *A Woman in Pink,* heavily brushed reds and greens and blues, a weary subject set against foreordained disaster. Euphoria began to swell up as I admired the superb technique; and I would have sung if I hadn't been startled by the sudden whirring as the chair's motor hummed to life. She turned very slowly. I was overwhelmed by the exaggeration of every detail. Every feature—eyes, mouth, lips, forehead—swelled into a ghastly grin that, I now realize, was both the cause and the consequence of the question she put to me. I didn't hear it the first time. More exactly, I didn't understand. Her head was held up perfectly in that cagelike brace and she was paralyzed except for her fingers, with which she operated a small joystick that controlled the chair. "Do you think I'm beautiful?" she asked.

As I said, I didn't understand what she meant at the time. I was frightened and would have screamed and run away had it been within my power. She fixed me with that ghastly look. "Do you think I'm beautiful?"

All I could do was pantomime, finger to breast. Me? You're asking me?

She couldn't nod, but did something with her eyes that gave the impression of nodding. "You think I'm ugly," she rasped.

Again, me? You mean me?

Her eyes flickered again. There was nothing to be gained

by lying. But that was what I did. Against all my better instincts, I put on a vaudeville denial, washing the air with splay-fingered hands. No no no no. You have it all wrong. Then I swept an arm across the great expanse of the view and beat my fist against my chest to indicate that nothing in all creation could be ugly against the spectacular background of nature. But it was bullshit. She was ugly and she knew it and, rather than sit there while I Buster Keatoned my way through lie after lie, she turned her buggy around and rolled away.

My walkie-talkie squawked to life. "Caruso. Calling Caruso. Come in please. Over." And before I could acknowledge, I heard the same voice calling directly behind me. I twisted around to see Theresa and James Bond walking across the lawn. Then there she was, bending down to buss my cheeks.

"Caruso. Congratulations. A boy! I am so happy for you. Here. Let me look. Putting on weight. You look good, Caruso." She smiled slyly, then stepped aside to give me a clear view of James Bond. "My husband, Caruso. No! Don't get up. Sit. Sit."

"How are you feeling today, Professor?" said James Bond.

"Why the funny face, Caruso? You don't remember him? The walks in the park?"

"The flying drinking cups?" Bond cut in, touching the back of his head.

"Caruso! How about you? Are you happy?"

The question was, of course, purely rhetorical. I had always loved that about Theresa. She understood the value of a rhetorical question better than anyone. She also understood the difference between stylized, effervescent living, and the real work of life involving the sublimation of one's outer personality to the silence of remote, inner nature.

H.R. appeared and spoke to Theresa in Spanish. They agreed on something or other and then H.R. waved goodbye and left.

"We brought you a present," Theresa said. She sat down beside me. Her husband's face was now familiar to me, but I had no idea who he was.

"Congratulations, Dr. Taylor," he said, and held out a package wrapped in gold foil.

"Open it," Theresa commanded, and with a joyous wiggle made room for her new husband to sit down beside her.

First the walkie-talkies. And now—binoculars! I lifted them out of the box. Leica BN Trinovids! They were the best! My hands trembed as I turned them over and over in my lap and felt my stomach begin a forward roll of joy. No doubt about it, she was my favorite aunt.

"You like them?" Theresa asked.

"We figured they'd be useful up here," her husband cut in.

'There's more," Theresa said, and pointed to the box. I reached in and took out—oh no! Not a book!"

"You know it?" James Bond asked.

I shook my head. Underwear and socks would have been more fun.

"*Guide to the Birds of Eastern North America*," he said. "You can use it right here on this bench."

Theresa put a hand on his knee and I could tell by her white knuckles that she was squeezing it gently and with great fondness. Suddenly I was sad.

"Right over there," James Bond pointed to a tree just a short distance away. "See it? It's a flicker."

"Here. Use the glasses," Theresa said.

I held the glasses to my eyes and looked down the long tunnels.

"Not that way, Caruso!" Theresa took the binoculars and turned them around. "Like this!"

"It's still there. Second branch from the top. On the left."

I scanned and scanned but all I could make out was a blur of foliage and sky and the view of everything so close up only made me dizzy.

"Can you see it?" Theresa asked.

"Here. Let me have a look," said James Bond. I handed them over.

Theresa took her hand from his knee, reached across me and picked up the book. She thumbed through it. "There. That's it. It tells you everything. Just look at the pictures and compare."

I held the open book in my lap. I didn't get it. Was I supposed to look at the bird or the book?

Theresa saw my confusion. "I'm lucky," she said. "I don't need the book. I have James Bond."

"I still carry mine," said James Bond, passing the binoculars to me. "You never know when you might see something you've never seen before."

"But you told me you've seen every bird there is to see around here."

"I never said that."

"Jes you did!"

"You misunderstood me."

"What did you say, then?"

"That I've seen just about every species of bird native to this area."

"Just about. Just about. You see, Caruso? That's what it's

like living with a scientist. You have to be berry careful what you say."

"Not careful. Just accurate." James Bond smiled back, earning a peck on the lips that sent me shivering with sudden need. He then launched into a discussion of bird feathers and fashion, explaining how one could see plumage from all parts of the globe right in Manhattan, and how he collected antique hats for the plumage—robins, brown thrashers, bluebirds, Blackburnian warblers, grebes, greater yellowlegs, kingfishers, swallow-tailed flycatchers and, yes, even pileated woodpeckers.

"Hats!" Theresa laughed. *"Con alas de pájaro!"*

I wondered what she meant to say, if it had anything to do with the something that dies between the lips and the voice. I stared at her, wondering if she knew what that something was; but then decided she didn't. How could she? How could anyone so mesmerized by the sound of their own heart know what is lost in every utterance, or worry about the way an idea becomes caught in a word?

"You don't write notes anymore, Caruso?" Theresa asked.

I took some labels from my pocket to show her.

"What are these?" she asked, turning them over in her hand, then returning them to me. I peeled one and slapped it on her. She reacted with a start and James Bond put down the binoculars at last. Theresa read. "Petrarchan sonnet. Media. Beautiful eyes, famished need. Appliqués of ground glass, flower petals, horsehair, soil from Mount Ventoux. I don't understand, Caruso," she said, then let her husband read.

I peeled another and stuck it on the bench.

"I understand," James Bond said. "You make labels to put on things."

I nodded.

"Why don't you write notes?"

I shrugged. It would have been impossible to explain and I wasn't entirely sure myself. Part of it was that I had lost some dexterity in my hands, and had trouble holding a pencil. Part of it was that living among so many works of art had taught me the importance of labels and I was merely adapting to my new environment. Part of it was that words just didn't come out the same way anymore. It wasn't that I'd lost the facility, but simply wanted to find new modes of certitude.

It was getting dark. Theresa stood up and suggested we go back inside. H.R. appeared suddenly, as always; and as we made our way back to my place, James Bond said, "It sure is a pretty spot here."

"Very peaceful," Theresa said. "Much better than the city, eh Caruso?"

I couldn't agree or disagree but only think of wishes granted in large and small measure, and how the former is generally punishment and the latter generally reward. I had walkie-talkies, books, bath toys, and now binoculars. Somewhere among all those things lay the true gifts, but I didn't know what they were.

As we entered the building the woman in the wheelchair appeared in the corridor. Theresa was holding my elbow and together we stood against the wall to let her pass. She whirred by without slowing down, eyes fixed way beyond the source of all her goals.

"*Pobrecita,*" Theresa murmured, and shook her head. I noticed that she smelled like lavender. When we returned to my place H.R. reminded us that visiting hours would be over in fifteen minutes and asked if we needed anything.

"We'll find our own way out," Bond said, looking at his watch.

I sat in the Laz-E-Boy and watched as the two did what you do when there aren't any toys to play with and nobody wants to admit they're bored. Theresa went around touching things—"Jour desk. Jour kitchen. Jour closet"—but since I'd already labeled everything there wasn't anything left but to take exception with the names I used. She read the back of my chair. "Admiral Ballsy? Who is Admiral Ballsy?"

I pointed to myself.

Theresa smiled. "But why? What does it mean, Admiral Ballsy?"

If I hadn't been too tired, I might have gone to my IBM ThinkPad and typed out an answer for her. But how do you introduce your play self to someone who knows nothing about pirates and roguery and would think you'd gone mad?

"Mind if I look at your books?" Bond asked but before I could answer he levered my paperback straight down, examined the cover, the back, then glanced at me and hefted the book in a kind of awkward salute. Then he put it back and took down another. This he perused for a minute or two, thumbing through as if reminded of a long-lost interest he could no longer remember the reason for; then he replaced that book, glanced at his watch and said, "I guess we better get going."

"Sorry we came so late," Theresa said. She was sitting on the armrest of my ship.

"The traffic leaving the city was horrendous," said Bond.

"We would have been here an hour earlier if we hadn't gotten stuck."

Theresa leaned over and planted a kiss on my forehead. "It was good to see you, Caruso. And congratulations. I'm happy for you."

I felt, suddenly, made of fog; and when Bond took my hand to shake it I felt a chuckle escape but could not quite make out the source of it or see what the effect on my visitors was. Being in a fog is inconvenient, especially when you've got company and they're trying to say their polite good-byes. Then another chuckle broke loose and Theresa sat back down on the armrest and asked, "What's wrong, Caruso? Are you alright?" And then the fog was swept away and a medley of Leonard Bernstein songs ran through me, and I was carried off on a wave of euphoric melancholy as the music swelled and Betty Comden and Adolph Green's lyrics floated from my lips.

Where has the time all gone to?
Haven't done half the things we want to.
Oh well, we'll catch up some other time.

I caught my breath. Theresa leapt up and clapped her hands. "Did you hear that? Caruso! You can sing! Jaimie! I can't beliebe it. He can sing!"

"A regular Tony Bennett."

Theresa squeezed my face between her hands and kissed me again. "Ah Caruso! The whole time! Why you didn't sing before? Come on. Sing some more."

But my pirate asserted itself and I became embarrassed. Bond looked at his watch.

Theresa kissed me one more time and told me to take care of myself and congratulated me again, and said not to get up, they could see themselves out the door, which they closed gently as they left, and I listened as their voices faded away down the corridor.

When Paulette came in to turn out the lights she had to rouse me from the spell I'd fallen under. "Wake up, Sugar. Time to go to bed." She helped me through the routine, pausing to admire the new binoculars and book. "Ought to get plenty of use out of these," she said.

I nodded, afraid to agree or disagree with a woman whose life was dedicated to assisting in the slow denouement of the living. Pump and plump and swipe and wipe and swab and fluff and all the rotten work involved in saving one more place in line from now to never again. I was still in a singing mood, and although Theresa had left, the lyrics rattled around inside my head; and as Paulette waited outside the bathroom door for me to finish washing up and re-diapering, I released them at my reflection in the mirror. *Ah well, we'll catch up some other time*

"Professor Taylor?" Paulette called though the door. I held the edge of the sink, sucked another draught of air into my lungs and repeated *some other time*.

The door swung open and Paulette, beaming, clapped. "Sing it, Professor! Sing it!" And even though I was standing there in my extra-absorbents, she didn't close the door or get embarrassed but said, "Rumor was you could sing. And sure enough you can!" Then she helped me into the bedroom. As I struggled with my pajamas she went through the apartment tidying up and generally applying herself to the unity and order of my little netherworld. As I climbed into bed, I noticed tiny flashes of light at the periphery of my vision. Gradually, the flashes moved toward the center. Paulette said, "Goodnight, Professor Taylor. Get some sleep. Big day coming tomorrow," and when the last light went out beside my bed I found myself floating in perfect silence among the rising stars.

When you're classified A2 you get a refrigerator so you can fix your own Cheerios and milk for breakfast like the zoon politikon that assisted living likes to pretend you to be. You can't vote because the institution hasn't arrived at the democratic stage yet, but it's not complete dictatorship, either; and as long as you keep your chin strapped in and your kitchenette tidy you can quietly pursue the to-be-or-not-to-be of aesthetic living and not worry that some jack-booted technician is going to come and take away your privileges. It's not spelled out. None of it is. You have to discover the limits and boundaries of everything for yourself.

"Good morning, Professor," H.R. said.

I was sitting at my desk looking out the window for early morning signs of Turner in the landscape, and feeling about as mellow as one who has come to the end of a natural view of the world can feel—which is to say, I was still in my pajamas. "Did you sleep well?"

I listened as he inspected the breakfast leavings and assembled my morning meds. The radio was not on, which meant that I was not listening to NPR, and it slowly dawned on me that, not only did I have no need of it, but the plein air peace I seemed in the quiet grip of was the direct result of its absence. Normally, it was Middle East peace talks, military budgets and tax cuts every morning. But it occurred to me that I could still do the hokey pokey as well as any Emersonian Oversoul, and get down with my bad self without the help of pundits, commentators and human-interest pieces.

H.R. appeared beside me. "Your meds, Professor." He was holding a glass and a tray of pills. "Professor. If you don't mind. Your thumb?"

Hmmm. Hmmm. I nodded.

"Please take it out of your mouth."

Again, I nodded. Hmmm.

"Professor, please." H.R. took my arm and tugged. "Time to take your meds."

I looked at my thumb lying there in my lap, wet and cool in the air, its qualities imbued with substances more delicious than anything that had come my way, piecemeal and bit by bit, for as long as I could remember. I lifted it back up, hmmm hmmm hmmm, wanting only to be left alone with the view. H.R. Tugged it out again. "First this, Professor." He plucked a tablet from the tray and offered it to me. When my thumb passed my lips again he put the tray and the glass down. "Professor Taylor. Can you hear me?"

Hmmm. Hmmm. I nodded.

"Can you see me?"

Hmmm. Hmmm. I nodded.

"It's time for your medication. Do you understand?"

I nodded. Hmmm. Hmmm. Of course I understood.

"Then please, Professor. Take your thumb out of your mouth!"

We regarded each other for a time, not unaware of the transfiguring effect a grown-up thumb in a grown-up mouth has on all notions of adulthood, but just uncertain of the consequences. H.R. had to consider it from his vantage point as a member of the helping profession; whereas, for me, it was much more a question of necessity, and not merely empirical necessity based on compulsion, but an inner necessity flowing from inner nature and thus *absolutely* necessary, and identical with absolute freedom. I would have liked to recite Shelling, chapter and verse, to remind H.R. and all the members of the staff of assisted living that only he is free who acts according to the laws of his inner being and is not determined by anything else.

"Okay, then," H.R. said, breaking off our staring contest. "How about we start all over again? From the beginning."

I liked the idea very much and nodded enthusiastically. Hmmm. Hmmm.

"Alright then. I'll go out and come back in and we'll take it from the top."

Suddenly, I was alone again, set aside, crippled with my private vernacular. I wondered what it would be like to be attracted to young North African boys, like André Gide was; or go pigeon shooting; or live in India as a member of the lowest caste. I wondered how one might go beyond a privately determined subjectivity and partake of a more universal other. It was an embarrassing moment, made all the more so by the fact that it came to me as a full-scale, thumb-sucking epiphany. There was nothing Romantic about it.

I took my thumb from my mouth and examined it for clues. Seeing nothing but a red and slightly wrinkled digit, I replaced it, trying to imagine just exactly what reaching beyond a privately determined subjectivity and partaking of a more universal other might entail. And the more I tried, the more impossible the whole thing seemed until, at last, a counter-epiphany rose up and swamped the whole business, and left me floundering in a sea of metonymies, anthropomorphisms, critical discourses, and bibliographies, with nothing to fall back on but my thumb and the view from out my window.

"Good morning again, Professor."

I looked up and saw H.R.

"You ate a good breakfast, I see. Are you ready for your meds now?" He stood directly in front of my chair, holding the trayful of pills and an oversized plastic jug with a flexible straw protruding from the top. He offered me the jug and a moment later I was swallowing pills, overwhelmed by the thought of homelessness, of stepping into subway cars, shouting "Hey folks! I'm here to sing for you. One dollar will get you blessed. A twenty will get you into heaven!"

"Very good, Professor. Just one more and you're finished."

I swallowed the last pill, bloated from water and eager to get down to the orderly morning routine of label-making when H.R. said "Big day today, Professor." Before it could occur to me to wonder with he meant, he had pulled out Petrarch and began to read about feet that never touched the earth, clear, cool, lovely brooks, souls full of doubt, and scattering remains on flowers and grass.

It made me want to go outside. I pushed myself up from the Laz-E-Boy and began to gather my things. H.R. stopped reading, put the book away. "Need help, Professor?"

I had my shoes. I had my socks. I had my pants. I had my shirt. I had my cane. I had my jacket. But I needed a shovel.

H.R. watched as I searched the closet, the bathroom, under the bed. But there were no shovels anywhere.

"Can I help you find something?"

I looked around the room, gaze suddenly falling on the spoon in my cereal bowl. I picked it up and made a digging motion.

"Still hungry? You want something to eat?

No no no. I pointed outside.

"You want to go outside?"

I nodded.

"It's still a little damp. And chilly, too. Sure you don't want to wait until it warms up a little?"

No no no. I want to go now! Right now!

We were crossing the lawn, heading toward the bench, my usual spot, when I veered off in the direction of the rose garden. H.R. did not resist. I dropped to my knees at the edge of the flower bed and buried my spoon in the soft dirt.

"You want to dig?"

I ignored the question, focused on the task ahead, the glistening, perfumed earth, the dirt, the light flickering in dreams and dots.

"We need to talk to the groundskeeper," H.R. was saying. "I think you'll need to ask permission."

But everything was too transparent and wet with dew for me to stop and think of permission. It wasn't just earth, but sky and water and measureless light I was after. The great, the small, the coming and going. I stopped to pick up a worm, held it in my palm, expecting an atavistic oh yuck, but feeling instead a narrowed distance, a who-knows-but-that-you-cannot-see-me, little creature, I will come home to you. I returned it to the dirt, covered it with a few spoonfuls.

"Professor. I think you'd better stop now." H.R. crouched

next to me. "Here comes the groundskeeper." He pointed to the figure of a man wearing a large floppy hat striding toward us.

"You're not digging up my roses, I hope," the man said.

H.R. began talking. The man peered at me and said something back, but I could not follow their conversation or make out anything more than my own blackened hands, the pungence of newly upturned earth, and the way my name was passed between them like something excessive, exquisite, and twenty years behind the times. I had no idea that butterflies could live so long into the autumn. I had not thought about roses blooming into winter, either. As the two men conferred, my attention wandered, but was suddenly arrested by the sight of small labels sticking out of the ground. I crawled forward for a closer look. Yes. They were labels. They were everywhere! And not just words, but pictures, too! Each was attached to a little wooden stick, and jauntily placed near the base of each plant; not my work but, evidently, the work of a more meticulous and much vaster nature.

"Whoa there!" Came a voice from behind. Suddenly the man with the floppy hat was squatting next to me. "Careful there, my friend. That's my nicest Mister Lincoln." He pointed to the bush. "Smell 'em?"

I retreated back to the grass. H.R. slipped his hands under my arms and hauled me to my feet.

"These here are all hybrid teas and shrubs mixed together." He pointed and began to name names. "Sarah van Fleet. Charlotte Armstrong. Pink Groatendorst. Miss All-American Beauty."

H.R. dusted the dirt from my knees and said, "We'll have to find another place for you to dig, Professor."

"Unless you want to do some weeding. I can always use help with that, you know," the gardener cut in.

Help? Me help? I nodded furiously. Yes yes yes. I want to help!

The man smiled and picked up my spoon, then spoke to H.R. "It's alright by me if it's alright by you," he said and filled in the hole with his foot. Then he spoke to me again. "This won't do you much good, I'm afraid. If you want to help me out we're gonna have to get you some real tools." He grinned at me and winked.

I nodded yes yes yes. Get me some tools. Real tools! I want to help! I'll be a good helper. Really, I will. And I wanted him to know that I'd be a good helper because I understood *exactly* what he needed! But what came out instead were the opening lines of "A Quiet Girl" from *Wonderful Town:*

Alright! Good-bye!
You've taught me my lesson.
Get mixed up with a genius from Ohio!

—which came out in a long forward roll of the diaphragm. Before I was finished, the man's hat was off, slapping against his dusty knee, and he was laughing and shaking his head. "By god, it sounds like you came straight up here from Broadway!"

H.R. was not so much amused as concerned. "I think we need to go back inside, Professor. Are you feeling alright?"

I nodded, feeling giddy. H.R. walked me back inside, but rather than go to my place, he took me to the main gallery. It was near the front entrance, a space devoted to temporary exhibits, where the artwork mingled freely, settling here and there, each to radiate its own uniqueness and stylistic development. He deposited me in a chair and told me to wait for him. There were a few things requiring his attention. My apartment was being cleaned. I had no choice but to accept this little bit of realism, and settled back as comfortably as the dying are permitted; lifted my legs up onto the ottoman, and gave myself over to the casual observation of the concrete historical problem and the quiet chaos of the club room. This was home, according to the brochures; in the sociological sense of *Gemeinschaft,* a publicly accessible sphere where rational consensus is advanced and strategic relationships pursued, and far and near corroborated with gentle pecks on the cheek and promises of frequent and longer visits from the closest to the most distant particles of the thermonuclear family. It was hard not to feel parched by all the surrounding need, which even among the most completed of the unfinished works, was always on permanent display. Even the self-contained ladies playing cards at the table tucked into the far corner of the room were fairly lit up with need, though I couldn't distinguish anything particular in it beyond a simple wish for company and a way to pass the time.

Presently, I became aware of someone next to me. I turned to see a deflated sack of a man in the chair beside me. He was offering me a Life Saver, and kept his eyes fixed directly on me as he bade me take one of the little candies. Were it not for the fact that this was assisted living, I'd have sworn the man was a day of the week, probably Sunday. I accepted the proffered candy, which I instantly regretted—not because taking candy from a stranger is a no-no, but because it launched him into a monologue, the outlines of which were that, far from being a Chestertonian anarchist, he was running for the Senate on the Republican ticket and had left his campaign on his boat someplace along the Intercoastal Waterway. His grandson was fine, just fine, thank you. Nothing that a little talk with the dean wouldn't fix. "Aren't you going to eat your candy?" he suddenly wanted to know.

I looked at the little disk, but could not have eaten it if I'd wanted to. With the wasties, and in spite of a Hyperborean, transworldly will to power, it was a choking hazard. And so, with great humility, and thumb securely between my lips, I offered it back.

"What's the matter? You don't like wintergreen?"

I nodded. Hmmmm. Hmmmm. A puzzled look came over him and he seemed about to ask for clarification, but then seemed to reconsider. "Keep it," he said, and resumed reading a magazine he'd been holding in his lap.

Thumb-sucking unscrambles all the complicated and acquired knowledge of old age and returns the intuitive wisdom of the child. This had occurred to me some time before, but the full glory of the discovery was not revealed until the man who looked like Sunday signaled his discomfort over the practice. It began with sidelong glances and a not-so-gentle turning of the magazines pages. But I didn't become aware that I was staring at him until he dropped the magazine in his lap and said, "Would you mind not staring at me like that?"

It hadn't occurred to me that I had been looking at him, or at anybody, for that matter. The expression on his face was aggressive and rude, so I averted my gaze and looked down into my lap, holding onto my thumb now for every bit of solace it could offer. I thought of the roses outside and the labels and all the names the gardener had called them.

The strain of his talk with H.R. began to come together, and terms like hybrid teas and repeat bloomers and grandiflora, floribunda, shrubs and climbers cycled in my thoughts as my tongue cycled around the thumb between my lips, happy childhood itself. There was really nothing to think about, and no place to go. I was happy, yes I was, happy just to sit there looking at the creases in my pants and at my feet propped up on the ottoman and do what every man of learning eventually must do, which is shut out its loathsome influence on the feelings that bubble up from your heart.

"Can I get you anything this morning?"

I looked up and saw a young woman I recognized, but could not place.

"I tried giving him a mint," Sunday remarked. The woman glanced at him, then asked again if I wanted anything.

"It didn't work," Sunday said. "He won't stop. Just keeps making that disgusting noise."

The woman smiled at him, but her focus remained on me. "Would you like to go back to your apartment?"

I wasn't sure; and became confused. I searched my pocket for some labels, but didn't have any with me, and felt the first tears rolling down my cheek.

"I can help you back, if you'd like," the woman said. But as she spoke H.R. came hurrying up.

"Hello, Professor. It's time now." He and the woman exchanged glances, and he said, "Is everything alright?"

"I was just offering to help him," the woman said. She put a tissue in my hand while H.R. explained something to her and Sunday watched like a man interested only in sticking to the facts.

It was good to return to my little lair, not the *Geheim-nisvolle*, inward *Weg* of mystery, a grown-up world filled with watching eyes, but to quiet, happy childhood in all its apparitions and destinies. There were flowers on my table. Roses. Freshly cut. And there were other incongruities and surprises scattered around the little room. I didn't notice them all at once, but only gradually which, I've come to see, is the nicest way for any experience to unfold.

"Fresh from the garden," H.R. said. "The groundskeeper cut them just for you."

I looked around. Everything was neat and in its place. My little IBM ThinkPad, my label printer, the shelves of books I could not read, my Motorolas and Leica BN Trinovids. H.R. showed me to the kitchenette counter where he'd put a big silver tea service with cups and saucers and a stack of plates and spoons and forks and napkins and little dishes with cookies. I wondered at first what they had to do with American landscape, the Hudson River School, my general idea of home, but before I could get to that, other empirical observations began to intrude. There was music coming from the radio. Not NPR news, but Bach's *Goldberg Variations*, turned just quietly enough so that if you strained to listen, they'd be too loud.

"I figured something soothing," H.R. explained, and opened the refrigerator to show me the pitcher of fresh-squeezed orange juice, milk and a demi-bottle of champagne. He held it up, and said with a wink, "Veuve Cliquot. In case you feel like a little celebration."

My first instinct was to begin making labels for all these new surpluses so I could remember what they were. I sat down at the computer and began to type. H.R. stood next to me, put a hand on my shoulder. "Professor," he said. I glanced up at him. "If you need anything just call me, okay?" I leaned on the table with half my weight, and H.R. put both hands on my shoulders and we looked at one another in an instant of brotherhood—H.R. of the greying Mexican variety, representing nothing I could name beyond an outline of underpaid machismo; and superbest, wasted me, the very soul-picture of a Green-backed Spotted Mossbunker.

And then there came a quiet knock at the door. Since nobody ever knocks in assisted living, I ignored it, and sat down to work out a label that was bursting to be written. In my glossary, the term for "club room" is "never-more-lonely-than-in." But before I could get the phrases to line up, the door opened and Gina appeared.

She was plumper of face and shorter of bang and lighter of brow and step. She was loaded down with a large shoulder bag and big plastic basket, which she held in the crook of her arm. She entered hesitantly, beaming, and put the basket gently down on the floor. Then she put the bag down next to it, marched over and held my head tightly to her, crushing my face against her and making it impossible to breathe. I felt her belly undulate once, twice, and she sniffled, choked back a little sob. Then she let go of me, sniffled again, took my arm and pulled me to my feet. Then she changed her mind, pushed me back down in my chair, and returned to the big plastic basket. I watched as she fumbled with coverings and straps and buckles, wondering how gentle one could possibly be with so much engineering in the world. At last, she lifted up a small bundle, and brought it over to me. "Meet Michael Taylor," she said, cradling the infant for me to see.

A familiar euphoric roll began someplace deep inside my

abdomen. Our gazes locked. I felt somehow as if the most basic and simple elements of nature had become lit by watchedness. There was no poetry, no talk of any sort here, but just a little shelter—a house, or even something more primal, like a shelter or a cave. I tried to hold little Michael Taylor's gaze for as long as I was held in his. I do not know how to describe him, and that made him all the more beautiful. We were wide awake, unfolded out of the folds; one silent, the other without language; everything in order, in its place, in need of nothing that our abundant hearts could not provide.

The undulation of my diaphragm completed itself. "Bofezars," I heard myself say.

"What was that, honey?"

It happened again, without music; just a single vocable. "Bofezars."

Gina sat down in the Laz-E-Boy, unbuttoned her blouse and, with practiced efficiency, guided the little mouth to her breast. "Bofezars?" she repeated as Michael Taylor's little body rested snugly against her.

I nodded. "Bofezars."

Gina repeated it, attention divided between the nursing infant and me. "Bofezars. Bofe. You mean both of ours!" She beamed. "Oh yes, Michael, Yes. He is. Both of ours. Our son." She glanced down again at Michael Taylor and adjusted him in her lap. Her gaze lingered on the little head, bobbing ever so gently now against her, and the tide of euphoria began slowly to ebb as each of us became absorbed in the *do-mi-so* of the living moment.

Outside, the gardener was pushing a wheelbarrow. I watched him cross the lawn and disappear behind a hedgerow. A few moments later the silence was broken by the loud revving of a chain saw and I began to think about helping out again and all the wonderful ways there were to build morale in a flowerbed.

"Michael? Are you sucking your thumb?"

I turned.

"Michael!" she started, but then broke into laughter.

I pulled once, twice, on the digit between my teeth, and smiled as best I could without removing it.

"Michael. It looks. You look." She broke off as Michael Taylor became momentarily detached. I could have finished her sentence for her, but became distracted when the woman in the head brace wheeled into view, doubling the tone in our little triad with a distant *do*. She rolled toward the bench at the far end of the lawn—*do-mi-so-do*—as Gina, with cheerful reluctance said "Cute," and quickly added, "But Michael, you have to admit, it looks a little ridiculous."

I pointed to the chair rolling across the lawn. Gina craned her neck, then sank back down to readminister her nipple. "Yes," she said. "I saw her coming in." Then, in a tone implying that nothing could detract from the lustre of the present hour, she added, "Poor thing."

Oh Gina! Oh motherhood! How square and straight and lofty. You could never offend. All your elements gathered together, indescribable, fruitful—and beautiful?

Yes?

Suddenly, I didn't know. Why not ugly? Why not both? After all, our perfect triad was not interrupted by the doubling *do* of the *Woman in Pink* in the wheelchair. It only grew more noisy. And yes! Of course! She was beautiful! She was absolutely positively beautiful. I began to feel my diaphragm revving with the motor of the chain saw, began bouncing my leg in time to a nervousness welling up, the fear that all will be taken away. I pulled the thumb from my mouth, turned away from the window and tried to focus my attention on Michael Taylor, whose tiny body was draped over Gina's shoulder, infant legs scrambling for purchase.

"What's the matter, honey? Is something wrong?" She patted the baby's back.

I didn't know. I couldn't know, and would have dodged any temptation to pretend otherwise. I glanced at the roses on the counter. They were only there to be admired and would also go away too soon. The revving saw and my bouncing leg began thrumming in unison and my next great thoughts were not of all the farms and cities in America and fatherhood and that all would soon be better, not the full moon rising over fields, but the infinity of time and the terrible laws of nature. Gina lifted Michael Taylor from her shoulder, patted him, slump-backed on her lap. The sight of that helpless, bald-headed little being calmed my philosophizing leg. Then, suddenly, a copius stream of white vomitus gushed from his mouth, and I was on hands and knees, scrambling across the floor to save him.

Gina laughed. "It's alright, Michael. Only a little spit-up." She wiped the little mouth with a cloth, then stood up to help me from the floor. "He always spits up a little after nursing. All babies do."

He does? They do?

"It stops after a few months." She pointed to the smears and stains on her blouse. "For now I'll go around looking like a Jackson Pollock." She put Michael Taylor back in the little carrier and helped me into the Laz-E-Boy. "And that little noise he makes when he nurses? It's an immature trachea. He'll stop that eventually, too."

Then she began setting up a tea party, talking calmly to

me about things I could not latch onto completely, the gist of which had to do with the experience of childbirth and what it was like to go places now with an infant strapped to you. "I take him with me everywhere," she said, and demonstrated a harnessing device she took from her big shoulder bag. All I could think was how pleasant it would be to climb inside it myself; and the more she talked, the more I wished to join Michael Taylor as the other closest thing in her company. We would be three things lost together, *do-mi-so,* lingering here and there as the desire moved us, covering ever greater distances together as our spans of time narrowed and narrowed until, one by one, each in their turn bade the others good-bye and faded away. But as Gina talked, I understood that she had already bid me good-bye, that I was now, at best, a calendrical feature to be visited and looked back bemusedly upon, never part of, but always athwart their life together.

"Oh look, Theresa's present." Gina examined the binoculars, then stood at the window, scanning the horizon. "She told me all about her visit. Isn't it wonderful? That they got married? She sounded so happy. James Bond. Can you stand it? He really is a famous bird guy, you know." She handed me the binoculars and I held them to my eyes.

"Not that way, Michael," Gina laughed, turned them so that instead of a long tunnel and the whole distant 180-degree horizon, I was looking at the back of the woman's braced head. She began to move. The chair turned slowly and I watched as she piloted her way toward me, head lolling slightly, eyes fixed straight ahead. I panned away, then back again. The chair drew slowly closer. Her features came into view. No. She wasn't ugly. She wasn't the least bit ugly, just dimmed by helplessness; and as she ground closer and closer, even that helplessness did not seem so severe that it could block up all her passages, render her unfit for tenderness and affection.

"What's that?" Gina asked. She switched Michael Taylor to the other shoulder. "Did you say bunk baths?"

Yes! I nodded. Yes yes yes. Of course. For Michael Taylor and me. Bunk baths. Bunk baths were fun. If I had bunk baths you could spend the night and we could have snacks and play until late.

Then the telephone rang and Gina picked it up. "Yes we are," she said, and then put the receiver down and turning an enormous smile on me said, "Honey, I have a big surprise for you."

Just then the door opened and H.R. came in, followed by Paulette and a whole gallery of others including Mr. Langer and Julian Bloom, who was carrying a big cake lit with candles.

They began to sing Happy Birthday, but I could not sing with them, not because I couldn't sing anymore, but because something was missing and I didn't know what it was. I glanced around the room, from face to many-sided face, each radiating in its own way a vital innocence. I understood that the song and the cake and candles were meant to symbolize this innocence and draw me into it. I became confused. Then everyone clapped. Someone shouted "Speech!" and there was a moment of self-conscious laughter and more clapping. Then Gina presented the cake, its candles glistening keenly in her eyes. "Happy birthday, Michael," she said.

I leaned forward and felt the warmth of burning candles on my face. Someone said "Make a wish," but I knew better, and basked for a moment in this and no other place. Then, slowly, I drew in my breath and all the coagulations of the past that trailed behind me, like the tail of a comet. I saw children playing at the seashore, spading sand into buckets. A regatta of sailboats sped along the horizon, and I was there too, skimming along the surface of moment to moment, admiring the trim of the sail, proud to be at the wheel. Then I was on the shore again, and on the boat, and on the shore. There were voices, but none distinct. There were faces, and all were distinct and I knew each one, but not exactly who they were. There were smells and sounds and, at the center of all these sensations, a miraculous self binding it all together, then flying apart, binding and flying and flying and binding in a haze that would like to be called memory but is more appropriately left undepicted. I saw a house, toys scattered in the yard, the comings and goings in the street, the songs of birds heard lying in bed of an afternoon, driving along a scenic highway in an old Plymouth that was new only yesterday. A gang of boys raced off the end of a dock while a portly man smoking a pipe watched from a wicker chair set in the middle of a broad lawn. Old wooden signs with the letters burned in identified cabins around a lake, the smell of pipe tobacco, a red-checked tablecloth and a woman's voice running down lists and lists and lists, reflective, retrospective, necessary and precious, of things to do today—not tomorrow, but today, because if they were put off until tomorrow they were certain to be forgotten. On the wall hung a calendar. The year was irrelevant; the point was to tick off the days, day after day, a neatly pencilled X in each box, culminating in birthdays, holidays and vacations coming up. If the past has a shape it is these Xs, all lined up in rows and columns, trailing one behind the other, one per yesterday.

I felt a sudden breeze at my back, and lifted my eyes from the blazing cake to the faces crowding all around. Words of encouragement were spoken. The air crackled with smiles and good intentions. I had the feeling that the door was open and people were continuing to arrive through it, but exactly who they were and where they came from I could not tell. I could hear music too, and the sensation of something opening up deep inside, not blooming or unfolding, but having to do with mirrors and lenses and the possibility of metamorphosis and transformation.

"Hurry up," someone said. "Before they go out." It was Gina's voice, but many-sided, unconnected with a particular biography. I felt myself straying back to all the places I have been but could not remember, exact places with names, imbued with their own special spirit, places where I once took up residence and lingered—all culminating and coming to an end in a momentary alignment of Inner and Outer.

"Hurry," came Gina's voice again.

I looked into the faces of all my favorite poems, arrayed objectively around me, pressing inward toward some greater idea. I saw the poets, too. They were singing, beating drums, walking, talking, flying through thunderclouds and rolling on. Gina appeared, leaned over the blazing cake, cheek to cheek. "Let me help you."

Julian hove into view, lifted a camera. "All three together," he said, and waved his hands. "A little closer," he said. I felt something being nestled in my lap. "On the count of three. One."

A glow spread from my face to someplace way before it, someplace primal and neither dark or light but simply— within.

"Two."

I looked up at Julian, standing there with the camera snugly against one eye.

"Three!"

The lights flickered, a warm wave of all the songs and poems I have ever heard played on. There was clapping. Shouts of Bravo! I looked down and saw that I was holding wide-eyed little Michael Taylor. And he began to cry.